ABOUT THE AUTHOR

Barbara Cartland, the world's most famous romantic novel-
ist, who is also an historian, playwright, lecturer, political
speaker and television personality, has now written over 530
books and sold over 500 million copies all over the world.

She has also had many historical works published and has
written four autobiographies as well as the biographies of her
mother and that of her brother, Ronald Cartland, who was
the first Member of Parliament to be killed in the last war.
This book has a preface by Sir Winston Churchill and has just
been republished with an introduction by the late Sir Arthur
Bryant.

"Love at the Helm" a novel written with the help and
inspiration of the late Earl Mountbatten of Burma, Great
Uncle of His Royal Highness The Prince of Wales, is being
sold for the Mountbatten Memorial Trust.

She has broken the world record for the last sixteen years
by writing an average of twenty-three books a year. In the
Guinness Book of Records she is listed as the world's
top-selling author.

Miss Cartland in 1978 sang an Album of Love Songs with
the Royal Philharmonic orchestra.

In private life Barbara Cartland, who is a Dame of Grace of
the Order of St. John of Jerusalem, Chairman of the St. John
Council in Hertfordshire and Deputy President of the St.
John Ambulance Brigade, has fought for better conditions
and salaries for Midwives and Nurses.

She championed the cause for the Elderly in 1956 invoking
a Government Enquiry into the "Housing Conditions of Old
People".

In 1962 she had the Law of England changed so that Local
Authorities had to provide camps for their own Gypsies. This
has meant that since then thousands and thousands of Gypsy

children have been able to go to School which they had never been able to do in the past, as their caravans were moved every twenty-four hours by the Police.

There are now fourteen camps in Hertfordshire and Barbara Cartland has her own Romany Gypsy Camp called Barbaraville by the Gypsies.

Her designs "Decorating with Love" are being sold all over the U.S.A. and the National Home Fashions League made her in 1981, "Woman of Achievement".

Barbara Cartland's book "Getting Older, Growing Younger" has been published in Great Britain and the U.S.A. and her fifth Cookery Book, "The Romance of Food" is now being used by the House of Commons.

In 1984 she received at Kennedy Airport, America's Bishop Wright Air Industry Award for her contribution to the development of aviation. In 1931 she and two R.A.F. Officers thought of, and carried the first aeroplane-towed glider air-mail.

During the War she was Chief Lady Welfare Officer in Bedfordshire looking after 20,000 Service men and women. She thought of having a pool of Wedding Dresses at the War Office so a Service Bride could hire a gown for the day.

She bought 1,000 secondhand gowns without coupons for the A.T.S., the W.A.A.F.s and the W.R.E.N.S. In 1945 Barbara Cartland received the Certificate of Merit from Eastern Command.

In 1964 Barbara Cartland founded the National Association for Health of which she is the President, as a front for all the Health Stores and for any product made as alternative medicine.

This has now a £650,000,000 turnover a year, with one third going in export.

In January 1988 she received "La Medaille de Vermeil de la Ville de Paris", (the Gold Medal of Paris). This is the highest award to be given by the City of Paris for ACHIEVEMENT – 25 million books sold in France.

In March 1988 Barbara Cartland was asked by the Indian Government to open their Health Resort outside Delhi. This is almost the largest Health Resort in the world.

Barbara Cartland was made a Dame of the Order of the British Empire in the 1991 New Year's Honours List.

Stand And Deliver Your Heart

The Earl of Wynstock is expected back from the Army of Occupation where he has been with the Duke of Wellington since the Battle of Waterloo.

He is, however, held up in London, not only by the Prime Minister and various officials, but also by Lady Caroline Standish, who is determined to marry him.

Only at the very last minute does he realise the danger and rushes away to the country.

Vanda Charlton has been waiting at Wyn Park, like all the other people on the estate, for his return.

The daughter of General Sir Alexander Charlton, she does not dare upset her father by telling him that a dangerous gang of Highwaymen have moved into the West Wing of the Earl's ancestral home.

She is terrified that they intend when the Earl does arrive to hold him to ransom, as they have done to a number of other people.

She therefore manages to meet him at the Inn where he will change horses before proceeding homeward.

He is persuaded somewhat reluctantly to ask the help of the soldiers in the Barracks not far from Wyn Park.

How the Earl discovers the soldiers are away on manoeuvres and he is persuaded to stay in the Barracks so that he will be in no danger.

How Vanda returns home to tell her father what is happening and is herself taken prisoner by the Highwaymen is told in this thrilling 437th book by Barbara Cartland.

BARBARA CARTLAND

Stand And Deliver
Your Heart

Mandarin

STAND AND DELIVER YOUR HEART

First published in Great Britain 1991
by Mandarin Paperbacks
Michelin House, 81 Fulham Road, London SW3 6RB

Mandarin is an imprint of the Octopus Publishing Group,
a division of Reed International Books Limited

Copyright © Cartland Promotions 1991

A CIP catalogue record for this title
is available from the British Library
ISBN 0 7493 0832 X PB
ISBN 0 7493 0941 5 HB

Printed and bound in Great Britain
by Cox & Wyman Ltd, Reading, Berks

AUTHOR'S NOTE

It was in the 18th century that the Highwayman became the greatest menace so that no main road was safe for a traveller.

But he was also thought romantic.

In actual fact, however, few of them were anything but the very worst type of criminal, who would murder or torture their victims.

There were, as I have told in this novel, a few wellborn Highwaymen, who came from respected families, and had been educated at Public Schools.

William Parsons was a Baronet's son, who was educated at Eton and was commissioned in the Royal Navy.

Simon Clarke was a Baronet in his own right, but became a Highwayman.

But they behaved better than Dick Turpin, the most romanticised of the Highwaymen, who was both brutal and unscrupulous.

Some Highwaymen escaped the gallows, but the majority were hanged at Tyburn which, until the end of the 18th century was the most uncivilised sight.

There would be thousands in the crowd assembled to witness the hanging: the Gentry sitting in the expensive seats which were close to the gallows.

The mob who could not afford the closest view, fought fiercely for the best places.

Spectators often had their limbs broken and some were even killed in the crush.

Apart from this, Tyburn was a Fairground with side-shows and street vendors offering their wares.

In 1789 the gallows were moved from Tyburn to the courtyard of the Old Bailey.

But a hanging was still open to the Public, and matters were not very much improved.

CHAPTER ONE
1817

Vanda rode through the woods thinking it was the loveliest day they had had for a long time.

There were primroses and violets peeping through their leaves under the trees, and the birds were singing.

She always enjoyed being able to ride in the great Park which encircled Wyn Hall.

Mr. Rushman had been the Manager of the Estate during the war.

He had given her permission to go there whenever she liked.

The old Earl of Wynstock was bed-ridden and his son was fighting Napoleon in the Peninsula.

"It would be nice to see someone young about the place," he said, "and there will be no need to take a groom with you."

That to Vanda was more important than anything.

Her father had insisted that she was always accompanied when she rode elsewhere.

They lived on the border of Wyn Park at the end of the village.

She had really only to cross the road under the trees to be, as she told herself, free.

She was thinking that it would be very frustrating now that the war was over.

When the Earl returned she could no longer use his grounds as if they were her own.

The young Earl, whom she hardly remembered, had come into the title three years ago.

He had distinguished himself at Waterloo and received the medal of gallantry.

He had then joined the Duke of Wellington's staff to serve him in the Army of Occupation.

Soldiers were demobilised and thousands began to return to England.

There was no sign however of the Earl.

"Perhaps he will never come back," Vanda thought happily.

She rode on towards the centre of the wood where she knew no one but herself ever went.

There closely surrounded by trees was the remains of an old Chapel.

It had once been used by a Monk who retired from the world to minister to the birds and wild animals.

He was a very holy man and there were all sorts of legends in the countryside of the animals he had healed.

Foxes which had been caught in a trap would have died had he not placed his hands upon them.

Cats and dogs that were injured and birds with a broken wing or leg were taken to him, usually by children.

He prayed over them and gave them his healing touch.

They left, so the legends said, stronger and better than they had ever been before.

The tiny Chapel he had built for himself had fallen into disrepair.

The villagers believed he haunted the wood and were afraid to go there.

"How can you be afraid," Vanda asked one old woman, "of someone who was holy?"

"'E were holy right enough," she answered, "but it be creepy-like aseeing th' dead."

No one in the village would put a foot inside Monk's Wood, however often they went in the others.

Vanda knew the boys went there to poach!

She thought personally they did very little harm.

With the Earl away at the war there was no one to shoot the pheasants and pigeons.

Nor for that matter the magpies and jays which the Game-Keepers thought of as vermin.

For Vanda the woods were therefore very much more enjoyable.

She loved being alone so that no one could disturb her.

She listened to the buzz of the bees, the rustle of the rabbits in the undergrowth, and the chatter of the red squirrels searching for nuts.

Sometimes too she thought she could hear music which came from the trees themselves.

She tried to compose it into music that she could play on the piano.

Her mother had been an exceptionally good pianist and Vanda had tried to emulate her since she was a child.

She was thinking now that she should compose a song of Spring.

She knew that the trees were giving her inspiration.

The wind moving the green leaves was creating a melody that she must try to remember.

Then suddenly she heard a strange sound.

It interrupted her thoughts and somehow seemed alien and coarse in the beauty around her.

There was another sound and she drew in her horse.

Her father always had exceedingly good horse-flesh in his stable.

The horse Vanda was riding was called *Kingfisher* and was her favourite.

Kingfisher responded immediately to her pull on the reins and came to a stand-still.

Vanda realised that ahead in the very centre of the woods, where she had never seen anyone before, there were men.

The sound she had heard was a coarse laugh.

Now listening she could hear voices and she knew immediately that they did not belong to local men.

The inhabitants of Little Stock – as the village was named – spoke with a slow but distinct Wiltshire accent.

Sometimes she laughed with her father at what they said and the way they spoke.

But she thought actually that it was quite attractive.

Whoever they were ahead in the wood were talking harshly.

Their accent was quite different and there was something about the sound of their voices that she did not like.

In fact she felt unaccountably afraid.

Who, she asked herself, could possibly be making so much noise in the one place in the wood that many people thought was holy?

She supposed they must be village hooligans, but from what village?

How dare they trespass in the private estate of the Earl of Wynstock?

These were unanswerable questions, and she knew it would be a mistake to try to find out the answer.

The laughter came again, then a chatter of coarse voices.

She could not understand what was said, but she was sure there were three or perhaps more men speaking.

She turned *Kingfisher* round and went back along the moss-covered path by which she had come.

When she could no longer hear the strange sounds behind her, she felt angry that the privacy of the wood was being violated by strangers.

She wondered what they could be doing there and why they found it so amusing.

"I shall never know the answers to those questions," she told herself. "But I hope they will go away and never come back."

It suddenly struck her that they might do damage to the great House itself.

Wyn Hall was a magnificent example of the work of the Adam Brothers.

It had been completed in the middle of the last century on the site of a much older house.

The Earls of Wynstock dated back to Henry VIII.

They had grown more important down the centuries and each one had improved the house in which they lived.

They had also bought more land.

Having been brought up in the shadow of Wyn Hall, Vanda had a deep affection for it.

In the same way she loved the old Earl.

He was a distinguished man who enjoyed the company of her father who was nearly the same age as he was.

The Earl had never been in the Army, but he liked to hear of the life Vanda's father, General Sir Alexander Charlton, had lived.

He told him about the years he had spent with his Regiment in India and how well it was doing under Wellington.

When the Earl died, Vanda knew that her father felt lost without him.

He had been shattered by her mother's death and when she was no longer there he was like a man who had been crippled.

He was however able to forget his unhappiness when he had a friend of his own age to talk to.

Now she thought sadly he only had her.

Although she tried to fill the gap in his life, it was difficult to do anything but listen when he talked.

Fortunately "The General" as the village called him, was now writing a book.

It was taking him a long time because he had so much to remember and so much to record.

At least, Vanda thought, he had reached the year when she was born.

She was certain that when it was finished it would be of great interest to the public.

She had actually had great difficulty in persuading her father to write down the stories he told so amusingly.

Her mother had loved them all.

"Tell Vanda," she would plead, "how you quelled a mutiny among your sepoys."

Or else she would say:

"Describe the beauty of the Palace belonging to the Maharajah of Udaipur and the pink one you liked the best in Jaipur."

Vanda adored her father's tales.

She knew that the task of writing his reminiscences was making all the difference to his life.

14

He had been writing when she left the house, and he would not realise how many hours she was away.

It was only for the last eighteen months that he had been unable to accompany her on horseback.

At first she felt guilty, knowing how much he enjoyed being on one of his well-bred horses.

Sir Alexander's legs were however swollen with rheumatism and it hurt him to walk, let alone ride.

Vanda reached the end of the wood.

She wondered if she should go home and tell her father about the strange men in the centre of it.

Then she had a better idea.

She would ride up to the Hall and tell the Caretakers to be on their guard.

If the hooligans were intent on making trouble, they might stone the windows.

Or, perhaps, try to break some of the stone statues in the garden.

"I will warn the Taylors," she decided.

She rode *Kingfisher* quickly through the Park under the ancient oak trees, across the bridge which spanned the lake and into the stables.

She was so used to going there that it was almost like coming home.

As she reached the Yard the Head Groom, who had known her since she was a child, came out of the stable.

He smiled a greeting before he said:

"Aft'noon, Miss Vanda, t'be a sight fer sore eyes t' see thee."

"Thank you, I hope you are feeling better and that the cut on your hand has healed," Vanda replied.

"It 'ealed immediate after yer tells Oi wot t' do with it," the Head Groom replied.

He took *Kingfisher* from her and led him into a stall.

Vanda walked along the path through the big banks of rhododendrons which led to the kitchen-door.

She did not knock, but went along the flagged passage to the kitchen.

It was a very large room with a high ceiling.

There was a large beam on which there had hung in the past game and dried hams.

Now there was nothing on the beam but one small rabbit.

The Caretakers were sitting at the large deal table drinking tea.

Taylor would have got up when Vanda appeared, but she said quickly:

"Do not move, I only came in to tell you something."

"Now ye sit doon, Miss Vanda," Mrs. Taylor said, who was a large rosy-cheeked woman. "I'm sure ye could do with a cup o' tea an' Taylor an' me were ajust having one."

"I would love a cup of tea," Vanda replied.

She knew it was what they expected to hear.

Although she did not really enjoy the strong, dark Ceylon Tea, they would have been disappointed if she had refused.

When it had been poured out and the cup was beside her she said:

"Such a strange thing has just happened. I was riding in Monk's Wood, and what do you think was right in the centre where no one ever goes except myself? There were men!"

She paused. Then as Mr. and Mrs. Taylor did not speak she went on:

"They were strangers and they certainly did not come from Wiltshire. There were quite a number of them, laughing in what I thought was an unpleasant manner."

It was then that she was aware that Mr. and Mrs. Taylor were looking at each other.

She felt, though it seemed incredible, they were not surprised at what she had just said.

"They be in Monk's Wood?" Taylor said at last very slowly. "Now what do ye think they'd be adoing there, Mother?"

He looked at his wife as he spoke.

She did not answer but seemed to be busying herself pouring more tea into her cup.

Although it was already nearly full.

Vanda looked from one to the other and then she said:

"Have you heard of these men before?"

"No, no," Mrs. Taylor said quickly. "We knows nothin' about 'em."

She was obviously agitated and spoke in a way which was not in the least like her.

Vanda looked at Taylor.

She did not speak, but he was well aware she was asking him a question.

"I knows o' nothin' us can tell ye, Miss Vanda," he said at length. "They 'as nothin' t' do with us."

"But you are aware they exist," Vanda insisted. "Have they been here causing trouble?"

Mrs. Taylor put down the tea-pot and laid her two hands palm-down on the table.

"Now listen t' me, Miss Vanda. Go home an' say nothin' of what ye've heard. There be nought ye can do about it an' us wants no trouble."

"Trouble?" Vanda asked in a bewildered tone. "What sort of trouble are you talking about, and how can it possibly affect you?"

Mrs. Taylor looked helplessly at her husband.

"We be alone 'ere, Miss Vanda," he said, "except

17

for the grooms, an' Goodrid be an old man while Nat an' Ben be high on a horse but small on th' ground."

Vanda would have smiled at the description of the two younger grooms, who did in fact look rather like jockeys, if she had not been worried.

"What is going on?" she wondered. "And why are the Taylors so mysterious about it?"

When she thought about it there was really no one to tell.

Mr. Rushman, the Manager, was over seventy and could no longer ride a horse on the estate, but drove a gig.

He was not in good health and in the winter was laid-up with bronchitis.

It kept him in his house week after week.

She pulled her chair a little nearer the table and resting her chin on her hands she said:

"Now tell me what is troubling you both. You know I will help if I can and, if you want me to remain silent, I will say nothing to anybody."

Taylor looked at his wife.

Mrs. Taylor gave a big sigh which seemed to shake her whole fat body.

"We'll tell ye," she said at length, "but I be too 'fraid t' speak o' them."

"Speak of who?" Vanda asked.

Taylor cleared his throat.

"It be like this, Miss Vanda. We be 'ere as ye knows to look after th' 'ouse till 'is Lordship comes 'ome."

"No one could do it better," Vanda said encouragingly.

It was true that with the help of three women from the village the house was as well looked after as when the old Earl was alive.

Granted there were not four Footmen in the Hall or a Butler in charge of them.

Nor was there a Chef in the Kitchen, the equal of the one employed by the Prince Regent, and three scullions under him.

When the Earl died, Mr. Rushman had appointed the Taylors as Caretakers.

They had lived up to that name and had taken the greatest care of Wyn Hall.

They had always in the past told Vanda how much they enjoyed their job.

She could not understand what could have occurred now to make them frightened and reluctant to talk of their fears.

"Go on," she prompted Taylor.

"They comes first about two weeks ago," he began.

"They?" Vanda asked. "Who are they?"

"That's what we ain't supposed to know," he replied, "but they be men."

Vanda knew that from the voices she had heard. She did not interrupt and Taylor continued:

"They asks for water an' they says t' the Mrs. an' I: 'ye keep yer eyes t' yerselves an' yer lips closed, an' no harm'll come t' ye.'"

"They said that!" Vanda exclaimed. "And what did you reply?"

"They be not th' sort o' men t' who ye'd make a reply," Taylor said.

"Then what happened."

"Don't tell 'er, don't tell 'er," Mrs. Taylor said in an agitated manner.

"I had much better know the whole truth," Vanda said, "and then if anything happens I will be able to help you."

"Nothing'll happen, nothing!" Mrs. Taylor said. "They promised that if us said naught."

"I do not count," Vanda said with an encouraging smile, "and I do not like to see you so upset."

"Us be upset right enough," Taylor said, "but there be nothin' us can do aboot it. Nothin'!"

"So where are the men?" Vanda asked.

There was a pause.

Then lowering his voice to little more than a whisper Taylor said:

"They be in th' West Wing, Miss Vanda."

Vanda looked at him in astonishment.

The West Wing had been shut up for a long time before the Earl died.

He had decided the house was too big and the West Wing contained a number of rooms which were never used.

In the East Wing there was the Picture Gallery, the Ball-Room, and a few bedrooms on the top floor.

The West Wing was just an accumulation of rooms of no particular historic interest.

Vanda thought the architects had built it merely to balance from the outside the other wing of the house.

At the same time it was definitely a part of Wyn Hall.

She could not imagine anything more horrifying than having hooligans, or whatever the strangers were, living in the house.

It seemed extraordinary that the Taylors had not gone to see Mr. Rushman and demanded that the men were turned out.

She knew, however, it would be a mistake for her to criticize their behaviour.

She therefore said:

"If they have threatened you it must have been very frightening. But surely they do not intend to stay for long."

"Us don't knows aboot that," Mrs. Taylor replied. "We just keeps ourselves t' ourselves an' pretends they bain't there."

"But they are trespassing," Vanda said quietly.

"Us knows that," Taylor said, "but they be dangerous, Miss Vanda, an' us 'ears tales o' things that 'ave 'appened which might 'appen 'ere."

"What sort of things?" Vanda enquired.

Again he lowered his voice so that she could hardly hear.

She was really reading the movements of his lips as he said:

"Murders."

"I do not believe it!" Vanda exclaimed. "And if these men are murderers, then how can we allow them to be here in the Hall and near the village?"

Taylor glanced over his shoulder because he was afraid that they were being overheard.

"Not so loud, Miss Vanda," he begged. "If anythin' 'appen t' thee we'd ne'er forgive ourselves."

"No indeed," Mrs. Taylor agreed. "Now ye say nothin' aboot it, Miss Vanda, an' per'aps they'll go away."

"And if they stay?" Vanda asked.

The Taylors looked at each other and she realised how frightened they were.

She wondered what she could say to comfort them.

At the same time she was trying to think quickly who could turn out these trespassers.

They had taken possession of an empty house with no one to protect it but two elderly people.

"I suppose," she thought, "it would be foolish to believe that something like this could never happen, especially after a war."

Men after risking their lives in fighting for their country had been turned out of the Services without a pension.

Even those who had been wounded or had lost a limb had no compensation.

Her father had been told what was happening in the Coastal areas.

Sailors dismissed from the Navy roamed the countryside in search of food and demanded money from quite humble householders.

"I can hardly blame them," Sir Alexander had said bitterly. "They won a war, but no one is concerned about them now that there is peace."

"Surely the Government should do something," Vanda had said hotly.

"They should," her father had replied, "but I doubt if they will."

They had gone on to talk about how the men who had fought came back to find their jobs had been taken by those who had stayed at home.

Many were lost altogether.

Now that hostilities had ended there was no longer the desperate need for food that there had been over the last fifteen years.

Farmers could not now sell their crops.

Also, a great many aristocratic land-owners had suffered financially from the war.

They could not employ the large numbers of staff they had been able to do before it began.

Tenants needed their houses repaired, but the landlords did not have the money to spend on doing it.

It was difficult to know where England could find purchasers of what goods were available.

"There must be somebody who could make these men behave," Vanda was thinking.

She felt she could hear again the sharpness of the voices and the rough way they spoke.

But she knew there were few men available in the village who could stand up to them.

Finally she decided it was something that she must discuss with her father.

He would know if there were any military in the vicinity.

If the worst came to the worst, they could get soldiers to turn out the intruders who were causing trouble.

"That is what I must do," she thought.

But at the same time she knew it would be a mistake to tell the Taylors what she intended.

"I can see you have been very brave," she said gently, "but at the same time it is something that cannot continue."

"Now don't ye be doin' anythin' aboot it, Miss Vanda!" Taylor said hastily. "If ye do, they might 'urt thee an' th' General."

"I doubt that," Vanda answered. "They can hardly come into the village, bursting into people's houses and beating up or murdering ordinary citizens."

"That be exactly what they will do," Taylor said stubbornly.

Vanda stared at him.

"Now you are a sensible man, Mr. Taylor," she said, "and you know as well as I do that we cannot have rough people taking the law into their own hands."

"This lot," Taylor said with the jerk of his thumb, "be abo'e th' law."

Vanda shook her head.

"No one is above the law and no one has the right to interfere with or to threaten ordinary citizens . ."

"Ye don't understand," Mrs. Taylor interrupted.

She looked at her husband and said:

"Ye'd better tell wh' they be."

"It'd be a mistake," Taylor replied sharply. Then he added:

"Well, as Miss Vanda knows s' much, 'er better understan' that unless 'er keeps 'er lips closed us'll be in trouble."

Again Vanda was staring from one to another.

She was trying to understand why they were so frightened and why they were so determined that she should do nothing.

She was suddenly afraid that these men might break into the rest of the house.

Wyn Hall was so beautiful inside.

She felt as if every piece of furniture, every picture, every book in the Great Library belonged in some way to herself.

She had known and loved them ever since she was old enough to appreciate such exquisite possessions.

Wyn Hall had become as familiar to her as her own home.

She knew that if any of it was damaged, it would break her heart.

Now she thought with horror of the miniatures which hung on the walls in the Drawing Room.

The portraits of the Wyns which hung on the beautifully carved stairs, the pictures in the Gallery which had been added to by every Earl.

She clasped her hands together.

"We must protect the Hall from these terrible people,"

she said. "Supposing they ransack the State Rooms, supposing they set the whole place on fire?"

"They'll not do that, Miss Vanda," Taylor said, "so long as us give them shelter. But if us turns 'em out anythin' might 'appen."

"They cannot stay here indefinitely," Vanda said.

"They'll go when it suits 'em," Taylor said. "They just want somewhere t' rest an' 'ide their 'aul."

"Hide their haul?" Vanda repeated. "What do you mean by that? What can they have to hide?"

They were questions that once again seemed to leave the Taylors silent and frightened.

In fact Vanda began to think that it was ridiculous.

Taylor was a well-built man. Why should he be shaking in his shoes when he thought about a few riotous young men who so far had done no harm?

"Now what I want you to let me do," she said in a soft voice, "is to talk to my father. You know how clever he is, and he has been a soldier all his life."

Mrs. Taylor suddenly gave a scream.

"Soldiers!" she cried. "If soldiers come 'ere they'll kill us. We'll both be dead, that's what we'll be, Miss Vanda, an' it'll be ye who's done it."

Vanda reached out to put her hand on Mrs. Taylor.

"Please do not upset yourself," she said. "The soldiers will not come if it frightens you, but we have to do something."

"There be nothin' we can do, an' that be th' truth," Taylor asserted.

"Just you go away an' forget us," his wife begged. "We be all right so long a' us do nothin'."

Vanda felt as though she was up against an insurmountable obstacle.

After a moment she said:

"Tell me where these men come from and who they are. Surely you must know that."

"Yes us knows that," Mrs. Taylor said in a whisper.

"Then tell me so that I can understand why you are so frightened," Vanda pleaded.

She looked at Taylor.

Once again he glanced over his shoulder towards the door as if he thought someone might come through it.

He then leant across the table and said:

"They be 'ighwaymen!"

CHAPTER TWO

Riding home, Vanda wondered what she could do about the Taylors.

They were obviously terrified of the Highwaymen.

They had begged her almost on their knees not to tell anyone about them.

Nor to try to remove them from the West Wing.

Thinking over what she knew about Highwaymen, Vanda could understand their fear.

She had often made her father tell her about the terrible menace the Highwaymen had been when he was a young man.

The most famed Highwaymen were a fraternity called "Knights of the High Toby".

A number of them, Hawkins, Maclean, Rann and Page, had all been in liveried service.

They therefore modelled themselves on their erstwhile masters and liked to be thought of as "The Gentlemen of the Road".

There were also, Sir Alexander had said, men who actually were gentlemen and had found it the only way to earn money.

"It must have been very dangerous, Papa," Vanda said.

"They nearly all ended up on the gibbet," her father replied.

"Were there real gentlemen who would do anything so outrageous?" Vanda enquired.

Her father thought before he said:

"Maclean was of good Highland stock and his father was a Minister. William Parsons was a Baronet's son, educated at Eton and commissioned in the Royal Navy."

"How could they have sunk so low!" Vanda exclaimed.

"Sir Simon Clarke was a Baronet in his own right," her father continued.

"It seems incredible that they should do anything which would make them outlawed completely from society."

"They certainly were that," Sir Alexander smiled. "But some of them retained the manners of their class."

"Who in particular?" Vanda enquired.

"James Maclean really deserved the title of a "Gentleman Highwayman," Sir Alexander replied. "He accidently fired his pistol and wounded the famous Horace Walpole in Hyde Park."

Vanda was surprised, but she did not say anything and her father went on:

"He was profoundly apologetic and sent Mr. Walpole two letters of regret."

"He at least was a decent sort of man," Vanda said.

"There were unfortunately a great many who were the exact opposite," Sir Alexander stated.

He thought for a moment before he said:

"Perhaps two of the worst were Captain James Campbell and Sir John Johnson, who abducted an heiress. She was only thirteen, but had a fortune of £50,000."

28

"What happened?" Vanda asked.

"They compelled her to marry James Campbell against her will."

"How terrible for her!"

"It was!" Sir Alexander said grimly. "Sir John Johnson was hanged for his part in the abduction, but James Campbell escaped to the Continent."

Thinking of these stories now, Vanda wondered what sort of men they were in the West Wing.

From what she had heard of their voices they might be as murderous and as terrifying as the Taylors thought them to be.

On the other hand, they might be led by someone better born and not so violent.

'Perhaps I am just being optimistic,' she thought.

They had certainly appeared very ferocious to the Taylors.

As she drew nearer to her home she decided that she must tell her father what was happening.

She must swear him to secrecy.

But she was quite sure that, however horrified he was by the situation, there was nothing that he personally could do about it.

Suddenly it occurred to her that if the Highwaymen were as bad as they were reputed to be, she and her father could also be in danger.

Theirs was the largest house in the village.

From a Highwayman's point of view, they were certainly wealthy.

Against a gang of armed men they had no defence whatsoever.

Besides her father and herself, there were in the house only Dobson and Jennie who acted as Butler and Cook.

Also Hawkins, who had been her father's batman.

Although he was getting on in age, he was indispensable.

Two women came in to do the cleaning.

But at night, now she thought of it, with the exception of herself every one in the house was old.

"If I do not tell Papa, whom can I tell?" she asked.

She felt she was carrying too heavy a burden.

Having gained the confidence of the Taylors she must try to help them in some way.

The difficulty was how to do so.

She took her horse to the stable where the two grooms, both over fifty, were looking after her father's horses.

They took *Kingfisher* from her and led him into a stall.

Vanda walked slowly to the house.

She was still undecided.

At the same time every instinct told her that she could not sit back complaisantly and just hope the Highwaymen would go away.

"I must discuss it with papa," she decided finally.

She walked into the Study and to her surprise her father was not at his desk.

Instead he was seated in one of the comfortable arm-chairs in front of the fire-place.

There was a book he had obviously been researching on his knees.

He was lying back with his eyes closed and Vanda realised that he had fallen asleep.

She stood looking at him.

Although he was still a very distinguished and good-looking man he was beginning to show his age.

His hair was almost white.

In repose there were lines from his lips to his chin that she did not remember noticing before.

"I cannot upset him," she thought. "It would be unkind. I shall have to think this out for myself."

She went very quietly out of the room shutting the door behind her.

Then she remembered Mr. Rushman. After all he was the Manager of the estate.

Although he too was old, in his position he could take action to preserve his Master's house.

Now she thought of it, she was certain that Mr. Rushman could appeal to the Lord Lieutenant.

Alternatively he could write to the Officer in charge of the Barracks which were not far away at Melksham.

"That is the solution," Vanda told herself triumphantly.

She knew she must go to Mr. Rushman at once.

There was no need to ask for *Kingfisher* again.

Mr. Rushman's house was inside the wall which encircled the Park.

She could walk there in under ten minutes.

Without bothering to change from her riding-habit, she went out of the front-door.

She entered the Park through the side gate she always used.

Hurrying along under the oak trees she came in sight of The White Lodge.

It was not really a Lodge, but had replaced one which had guarded a different entrance to the Park.

The Lodge had become a very attractive and comfortable house.

Mr. Rushman had lived in it with his wife since he was first appointed Manager of the estate.

Now his wife had died and he was alone.

Yet he seemed to be quite happy and there were always a great number of callers at The White Lodge.

There were villagers with their grievances over a leaking roof or a broken window.

There was also a number of people like the Doctor, the Vicar and Members of the Hunt who looked on Mr. Rushman as a friend.

The General was very fond of him and so was Vanda.

She thought now she had been very foolish in not realising that she should have gone to Mr. Rushman immediately.

Also she should have advised the Taylors that was what they should have done.

Mr. Rushman's Housekeeper, who was a very superior middle-aged woman, opened the door.

"It's nice to see you, Miss Charlton, and I'm sure Mr. Rushman'll be delighted."

She hurried across the hall without waiting for Vanda's reply.

Only when she reached the door into the Estate Office where Mr. Rushman usually sat, did she turn to say in a whisper:

"His legs are hurting him today and it's all the worse for him because, as he'll tell you himself, something important's happening."

"Important?" Vanda longed to question.

The Housekeeper had already opened the door.

"Miss Charlton to see you, Sir," she announced.

Vanda walked in.

Mr. Rushman was not at his desk, but sitting upright in a high-backed arm-chair with his legs raised on a stool.

He had a great number of papers and account-books arranged beside him.

He was writing with a large quill pen.

He looked up and smiled as Vanda walked towards him.

"You are just the person I want to see, Miss Vanda," he said, "and actually, I was just going to send a message to your father."

"What about?" Vanda asked as she sat down in a chair near him.

"I have news," Mr. Rushman said, "good news. But at the same time it would come when it is difficult for me to move."

"And what is your news?" Vanda enquired.

Mr. Rushman replied almost dramatically:

"His Lordship, the Earl, is coming home!"

. . . .

The Earl of Wynstock arrived in London.

It was a long time since he had been in England and everything had changed.

Not, he thought, for the better.

The streets were more crowded and there appeared to be a great number more beggars than he remembered.

He had not missed after landing at Dover the numbers of demobilised soldiers and sailors who were to be seen in every town at which he stopped.

They were lounging about with obviously nothing to do.

Or, in many cases, sitting despondent by the roadside, hoping against hope that somebody would take pity on them.

The Earl had heard, while he was still in France, that this was happening in England.

Now he saw it for himself, it made him very angry.

After fighting for five years against Bonaparte no one appreciated more than he the courage and the endurance of the British Soldier.

He had heard the same story from his friends who had been in the Navy.

It seemed appalling that the men who under Nelson and Wellington had saved England should be treated so shabbily.

He was determined he would speak about it as soon as he had the opportunity in the House of Lords.

He was, however, aware there would be a great deal for him to do once he arrived home.

First he must open Wyn House in Berkeley Square and Wyn Hall in Wiltshire.

The Duke of Wellington thought him one of the most able of his Officers in that he had a genius for organisation.

The Earl was sensible enough to be aware that was something he would certainly need in reconstructing his own life.

At twenty-nine so many of his years had been concerned with war.

He knew it would be difficult to readjust to a very different existence.

He had, in fact, found the gaieties of Paris almost overwhelming after the hardship and the danger of the battle-fields.

He had gone there with the Duke of Wellington from Cambrai, where the Army of Occupation was billeted.

He had felt at first dazzled by the notorious extravagant and fascinating Courtesans.

He was amazed by the way in which the French had

adjusted themselves overnight to peace after the defeat of Napoleon Bonaparte.

Paris was once again a city of pleasure, and the Earl would have been inhuman if when he was off duty he had not enjoyed it.

He indulged in several exhilarating and fiery affairs with the most sophisticated and experienced women in Europe.

Then he became involved with Lady Caroline Standish.

She was beautiful, exotic, and had stalked him as if he was a stag from the first moment she set eyes on him.

A widow since the age of twenty-one, she made the most of being related to a number of the greatest aristocratic houses in England.

It was influence that enabled her to reach Paris very shortly after hostilities ceased.

Because she was rich, the parties she gave for every attractive man in the British Army were much sought after.

They rivalled those given by and for the Courtesans.

The Earl was not quite certain how it happened, but he found Lady Caroline was with him wherever he went.

Without meaning to he met her practically every day.

It was on her insistence that it became every night.

It was only when it was almost too late that he realised that she was seeking not only amusement, but marriage.

One thing he had determined during the war was not to get married until he was very much older.

He had heard too much, not only from his friends, but also from the men he commanded, of unfaithful wives.

"I trusted her," a brother Officer told him bitterly, "not only with my house, my money and my children, but also with my heart."

He went on to tell the Earl exactly what had happened.

It was inevitably one of his relatives who had informed him in the first place of his wife's infidelity.

Because the Earl was a good Officer and his men trusted him, he learnt of their troubles also.

"Gone off with th' Inn Keeper, her 'as," his Seargeant-Major told him, "and me mother writes to tell Oi 'er has stripped th' house o' everythin' Oi bought for it."

There were innumerable men who had been cuckolded by their closest friends, besides the Carrier, the Landlord or the GameKeeper.

It was then that the Earl began to wonder if all women were untrustworthy.

He felt that a woman who took lover after lover was not a particularly admirable specimen of her sex.

He had never known his mother, whom he had adored, being concerned with any man except his father.

He told himself that, when he did marry, it would be someone who would love him and him alone.

He would kill his wife rather than share her with another man.

He would, however, have been inhuman if he had resisted Lady Caroline's experienced blandishments.

She entwined herself like clinging ivy.

It was only when there was talk of his returning

home that he realised he stood on the brink of a very dangerous gulf.

"I hope I shall be able to get away next month," he had said to Caroline.

They were having dinner in the house he had rented with another brother Officer while they were in Paris.

It was a bore to stay at the British Embassy with the Duke.

Hotels were practically non-existent and uncomfortable and sordid.

The house his friend had found had belonged to one of Napoleon's social upstarts.

They had been disdainfully ignored by the French of the *Ancien Régime*.

It was expensively furnished.

The servants who were in charge of it were delighted to have regular wages from two Englishmen who paid them punctiliously.

The Earl's friend was seldom in the house.

He therefore found himself continually having dinner alone with Lady Caroline.

He had to admit she looked very alluring.

As the daughter of the Duke of Hull she had taken London by storm the moment she appeared as a débutante.

She had made a good marriage in marrying a man who came from a family which was as blue blooded as her own.

He was also extremely rich.

When he was killed it did not perturb her unduly.

She had already found him dull, and before he was dead she had amused herself with several lovers.

Caroline Standish was wise enough to realise that her beauty would not last forever.

Her extravagance both in England and France had considerably eaten into her fortune.

She was, therefore, looking for a husband who was both rich and distinguished.

Who better than the Earl?

Her golden hair gleamed in the candle light.

Her gown which was in the high-waisted style, originally set by the Empress Josephine, was very revealing.

After the announcement that he would be going home, the Earl said casually:

"Will you be staying here?"

Lady Caroline's large blue eyes looked up at him in surprise.

"Surely, Neil," she said softly, "you know that I will be coming with you."

The Earl stiffened.

He had found Caroline extremely attractive.

But he had no intention of arriving in London with her as part of his baggage.

He knew that not only his houses were waiting for him, but his family.

He was well aware how much she would shock his Grandmother, Aunts, Cousins and all their friends.

There was silence.

Then Caroline said in a low seductive voice:

"I love you, and if I cannot live without you, I am quite certain you cannot live without me."

The Earl thought it was not the sort of conversation one should have at the Dinner Table.

When he had taken Caroline back to her house, he had very unwisely, he thought later, stayed with her as he usually did.

She had been far too experienced to continue the conversation which she was aware had been a shock to the Earl.

Instead she used every wile she knew to arouse his passion.

As she was very experienced and he was very much a man, it was not a difficult thing to do.

Later they were lying closely in the big canopied bed.

There was only a faint light from a cupid-fashioned candelabrum behind the curtains.

Caroline drew a little nearer.

"How could anyone," she asked, "have a more wonderful lover? My darling, we shall be very, very happy together."

The Earl who was practically asleep was suddenly aware of the danger.

He had been aware of it in the same way when he was on the battle-field.

He knew that Caroline had chosen this moment when he was at his weakest to press her suit.

With an effort he yawned.

"I must go back," he said. "The Duke wants me to breakfast with him."

Caroline's hands were touching him and her lips were very close to his.

"I want you to stay with me," she whispered. "I find it hard to lose you even for what is left of the night."

The Earl got out of bed.

"One thing I dislike," he said conversationally, "is having to discuss political strategy at breakfast."

"You are not listening to me," Caroline said petulantly.

"I am sorry," the Earl replied, "but I really am tired."

He dressed quickly.

Caroline watched him.

Lying back against the pillows, she looked as beautiful as a translucent pearl in a velvet-lined box.

The Earl moved towards the door.

"Good night, Caroline."

She gave a little cry of protest.

"You have not kissed me good night! How can you be so cruel?"

She stretched out her white arms.

The Earl was well aware this could be a trap which had caught many men unawares.

If Caroline were to put her arms around his neck, he would lose his balance.

He would fall on top of her which was exactly what she wanted.

He took her hands and kissed first one and then the other.

"Thank you for making me happy," he said.

Even as she cried out to prevent him from going, he shut the door behind him.

His carriage was waiting outside.

He drove back to his own house where he was staying.

He was wondering frantically how he could avoid being married to Caroline Standish.

He was quite prepared to admit it was his own stupidity which had made him so involved.

Already, and this was of course engineered by Caroline, people linked their names together in Paris.

Doubtless the gossips were also talking about them in London.

Too late he saw he should have prevented her from being always at his side and of course from talking.

What woman did not talk?

Caroline was clever enough to use public opinion when it suited her.

When he got into his own bed he was still asking desperately what he should do.

The question turned over and over in his mind.

His valet called him early the next morning and after a cold bath he dressed himself in uniform and hurried to the British Embassy.

To his relief he was alone at breakfast with the Duke.

They discussed several propositions which had come from the French.

They were doing everything in their power to reduce the size of the Army of Occupation.

Suddenly the Earl had an idea.

"I wonder, your Grace," he said, "if you would consider sending me back to London as soon as possible."

The Great Man looked at him penetratingly.

The Earl was aware that he knew he had an ulterior motive in the request.

"You want to go home?" the Duke asked.

"If it is possible for you to spare me."

The Duke considered this for a moment and then he said:

"I shall miss you, of course I shall miss you."

He smiled and went on:

"But I appreciate, Wynstock, that you could easily have refused to stay with me this last year, having an unanswerable excuse in the necessity of attending to your own affairs."

The Earl inclined his head and the Duke continued:

"I think I can guess your reason for wishing to be

gone, and if you take my advice you will leave without fond farewells, recriminations or tears."

With a slight twist of his lips, the Earl knew this was what the Duke often suffered himself.

Aloud he said:

"That is extremely kind of Your Grace. If I can do as you say, it will make it a lot easier."

"Very well," the Duke replied. "I order you to go to-morrow."

"Thank you," the Earl murmured.

"I will give you certain letters for the Prime Minister," the Duke said shortly, "and as they are of course secret, you can arrange your leaving so that no one is aware of your departure until you have gone."

"Thank you, thank you a thousand times," the Earl said again.

It was all much easier than he had anticipated.

Keeping secrets from the French had been well drummed into the members of the Duke of Wellington's Staff. As one wit said:

"I am afraid of my own shadow."

The Earl dined with Caroline.

Fortunately there were a number of other men present.

She was at her very best, holding everyone spellbound by her charm and wit.

She flirted outrageously with every man from the oldest to the youngest.

It was, the Earl appreciated, a glittering performance.

He was quite certain from the way she looked at him under her eye-lashes and pouted her lips provocatively, that it was all done for him.

She was demonstrating how she could entertain his friends.

If she could shine against an alien background, how much better at Wyn Hall?

Caroline had once been to Wyn with her father and had never forgotten it.

The Earl was aware that more than anything else she wanted to become its Chatelaine.

To sit at the end of his table wearing the Wynstock Jewels.

He left the party at nearly one o'clock.

He knew that Caroline was perturbed that he did not stay until the rest of her guests had gone.

"I have to be up early," he said truthfully.

He was aware that she thought it a parade.

Or that once again he was breakfasting with the Duke.

"Come to me as soon as you are free," she whispered.

Her eyes told him exactly what that meant.

When their relationship first started, he had found her exciting to the point when it was hard to think about anything else.

He had on several occasions, at her invitation, called on her in the morning.

She was certainly alluring with her golden hair falling over her naked shoulders.

She usually wore little except a necklace of emeralds or one of black pearls which enhanced the whiteness of her skin.

The Earl did not pretend for a moment that he had not been infatuated with her.

But an *affaire de coeur* was one thing, and marriage was another.

He could not imagine his wife, the Countess of Wynstock, receiving a man in her bed-room while the servants sniggered about it downstairs.

As he left Paris for Calais he knew he was running away.

However he told himself it was a wise General who knew how to withdraw in the face of superior odds.

He would live to fight another day!

As soon as he arrived in London, the Earl found there were a thousand things to do.

He took the secret papers to the Prime Minister.

The Earl of Liverpool wanted to hear a great deal about the Army of Occupation that was not in the reports he had received.

The Earl then decided he must call on the Prince Regent.

If he did not do so he would certainly be in the Black Book at Carlton House.

The Regent was delighted to see him.

The Earl was new and interesting, something which His Royal Highness was always seeking.

He insisted on his lunching, dining, and meeting his friends.

He asked the Earl to accompany him to the Race Meeting at Epsom, to a meal on Wimbledon Common, to a display of swordmanship at Gentleman Jackson's Gymnasium.

In between these activities, the Earl engaged servants to run the House in Berkeley Square.

He also bought a number of horses at Tattersall's Sale Rooms.

Invitations poured in as soon as the great Social Hostesses of London realised he was back.

There were, of course, also a number of old friends to meet at White's Club.

They too had suggestions for what he should see and who he should meet.

They told him of the pretty new ballerinas at Covent Garden.

The pleasures of the White House, which he had not enjoyed before he went abroad.

Who were the latest Incomparables whom he would be very stupid to ignore.

It was rather like Paris, but at the same time he found the Regent witty and undoubtedly amusing.

The soirées and the receptions were somewhat dull. The Incomparables not so fantastic or so fiery as Caroline.

Even to think of Caroline made him wonder if he had really escaped, or if she would follow him back to England.

When he had heard nothing for nearly a week, he thought optimistically that she had found Paris too exciting to leave.

Then, as he walked into his Club, one of his closest friends said:

"I have just been told a friend of yours is back in London."

The way he spoke and the expression in his eyes made the Earl draw in his breath.

"Who are you talking about?" he asked.

There was no need to listen to the answer.

"Caroline Standish."

The Earl instantly made up his mind.

"I will go to the country," he told himself, "and I will leave first thing to-morrow morning."

CHAPTER THREE

Vanda stared at Mr. Rushman in surprise before she exclaimed:

"The Earl is coming home? When?"

Mr. Rushman looked down at a letter which was beside him.

"His Lordship says," he replied, "that he will be leaving London on Wednesday which is today. That means he should be here on Friday."

Vanda made a little murmur before he went on:

"His Lordship asks that I send a pair of the best horses to the '*Dog and Duck*' at Gresbury."

He looked at Vanda and added:

"You know, Miss Vanda, as well as I do that we have nothing in the stable which His Lordship would consider worth driving."

Vanda knew this was true.

When the old Earl died, the horses were already getting on in years.

Gradually most of them were put out to grass.

What remained were only useful for the grooms to ride to the village to collect provisions.

She saw the worry in his face and said quickly:

"I know Papa would be delighted to send a pair of our horses to carry the Earl on the last leg of his journey."

"That would be extremely kind of you," Mr. Rushman replied, "as I am sure his Lordship wishes to arrive with a flourish."

He smiled as he spoke.

Vanda had the idea that he was thinking of the Earl as they had last seen him.

A young man of twenty-two, full of enthusiasm and a magnificent rider.

"There are a great many other things to do," Mr. Rushman went on, "for I expect His Lordship has forgotten that the House has been closed and the staff either dismissed or retired."

"Buxton is living in the village," Vanda said.

She was thinking of the Butler who had always been a very impressive, pontifical figure.

In the past the whole House had seemed to revolve around him.

"I have remembered that," Mr. Rushman said, "and thank goodness Mrs. Medway is alive."

"Do you think they will come back?" Vanda questioned.

"I am sure they will if you beg them to do so," Mr. Rushman replied. "They will at least be willing to oblige until we can get younger people to take their place."

"Me?" Vanda enquired. "You want me to ask them?"

Mr. Rushman made an eloquent gesture with his hands.

"When I received this note from a groom who had ridden post-haste from London, I was wondering who would help me and how I could reach Buxton and Mrs. Medway."

He paused before he added:

"I can, of course, try to crawl there!"

"You know I will do anything you want," Vanda said,

"and it will be very exciting to have Wyn Hall full and the Earl in charge."

"I am afraid things are not like they used to be," Mr. Rushman said sadly, "but the Taylors have done their best."

Vanda realised that in the excitement of hearing about the Earl's return she had for the moment forgotten the Taylors.

And in particular the reason why she had called on Mr. Rushman.

Knowing how much he now had on his mind, she felt she could not add to his difficulties.

After all, she thought to herself, if the Highwaymen refused to leave, there was nothing that he personally could do about it.

The Earl was returning and it would be up to him to protect his own property.

She rose to her feet.

"I will go and talk to Buxton and Mrs. Medway. I suppose they can employ anyone they wish from the village."

"Everyone on two legs as far as I am concerned," Mr. Rushman replied. "I can only pray that the house is not as dusty as I fear it may be."

"Do not worry about that," Vanda said. "The Taylors have been wonderful and the women who clean the rooms every week have kept it looking exactly as it did when the Earl's father was alive."

Mr. Rushman gave a sigh of relief.

"That is one burden off my mind, Miss Vanda."

Vanda smiled.

"Dare I ask you," he continued, "to see if Mrs. Jacobs is capable of taking over the kitchen until I can find a Chef."

"She is very old," Vanda answered, "but she could sit down and tell the others how things should be done."

She considered a moment then went on:

"Mrs. Taylor is quite a good cook and there are several women in the village who could help them."

"You are an angel from Heaven when I was almost in despair!" Mr. Rushman exclaimed.

"I expect that is where I will get my reward," Vanda laughed. "I will go and see the three important people concerned with His Lordship's comfort, and report to you later what they say."

"Thank you, thank you," Mr. Rushman cried. "And tell your father also how grateful I am."

Vanda hurried away.

She knew better than anyone else how much there was to do.

If the Hall was to be as comfortable and the Earl as well served as he remembered, they needed time.

She was only a little girl of ten when, after he had left Oxford, he had gone into the Horse Guards.

It was always known as the family Regiment.

He had come home perhaps twice the following year.

Then he left England and no one had seen him again.

He had, of course, written to his father who showed the letters to Sir Alexander.

Both men knew that the young Viscount, as he was then, was in the thick of the fighting.

When there were so many casualties it seemed almost a miracle, Vanda thought, that he had survived.

Yet he had, and she knew he would be horrified if he returned to find the House still closed, the Taylors almost incoherent with fear and Highwaymen in the West Wing.

While Vanda was thinking, she had been walking quickly towards the village.

She soon came to a small, attractive cottage to which Buxton, the Butler, had been retired.

It was, of course, a cottage which belonged to the Wyn estate.

It was in good repair and had been recently painted.

The garden was bright with Spring flowers.

As she walked up the path to the front-door, she wondered if Buxton would feel too old to do what was asked of him.

He opened the door.

She thought, although his hair was dead white, he looked in good health.

"This be a surprise, Miss Vanda," he said, "but, a very pleasant one. Will you come in?"

"Thank you," Vanda said.

She walked into a small room which was a kitchen and where Buxton habitually sat.

On the other side of the entrance passage there was a very small parlour.

It was kept for important occasions, and could hold no more than four people.

Vanda, because she knew Buxton would expect it, sat down in an armchair in front of the stove.

"I have news for you," she said. "His Lordship has returned to England and will be arriving home on Friday."

"Friday!" Buxton exclaimed.

"Yes," Vanda answered, "and Mr. Rushman, who is too ill to come and see you himself, has asked me to beg you to get the House ready for him."

She was watching the old Butler as she spoke.

For a second she thought he was going to refuse.

Then as he smiled she thought there was a light in his eyes that had not been there before.

"Be Mr. Rushman giving me a free hand, Miss Vanda?" he enquired.

"You can have anybody and everything you want," Vanda assured him, "and you know as well as I do that nobody could get the place ready but you."

"Very well, Miss Vanda, I'll do my best," Buxton said, "but I'll need a lot of help."

"Mr. Rushman's actual words were that you could have 'everyone on two legs'," Vanda replied.

Buxton laughed.

She knew she had won this battle at any rate.

Almost the same conversation took place in Mrs. Medway's cottage which was identical to Buxton's.

But being a women she needed more coaxing and of course more flattery.

"Who else but you," Vanda asked, "would know what sheets to put on the bed and make sure they are properly aired?"

She paused before she added:

"What is more, if you say no, I think Mr. Rushman will worry himself into the grave."

"Well I'll do what I can," Mrs. Medway said at last rather reluctantly. "I'm too old now to cope with them young girls who think they know better than I do."

This was an old cry that had echoed down the ages.

Vanda agreed with her that the young were uppish and not as respectful as they should be.

By the time she left, Mrs. Medway was calculating who in the village she would need to help her.

Vanda knew that with Buxton and Mrs. Medway

at the Hall the Earl would be comfortable when he arrived.

Then she had seen Mrs. Jacobs.

She agreed to go to the Hall if she could be taken there in a carriage.

It was only as Vanda walked home that the problem of the Highwaymen returned to her mind.

She wondered what she should do about it.

Then just before she reached her own home, she recalled a frightening story her father had told her many years ago.

A Highwayman, who she thought was called Watson, had tortured a Diamond Merchant into giving him half his fortune.

Watson and his accomplice had captured the merchant when he was returning to his house on the outskirts of the City.

They had taken him to an empty barn in the country-side.

There they forced him at knife and pistol-point to write them a cheque for many thousands of pounds.

Because Watson could make himself look quite presentable, the Bank had handed over the money without querying the size of the sum involved.

They had then decamped, leaving their prisoner tied up and helpless in an isolated spot.

It was only by chance that he had been discovered by some children.

He was alive but practically dead from starvation.

The tortures he endured affected his health to the point that he died two years later.

Both the Highwaymen had already been caught and hanged for the theft.

Vanda now remembered hearing that story among a

52

number of others, and thought it was very frightening.

She had forgotten it until this moment.

She wondered if the same treatment could possibly happen to the Earl.

Granted, there would be a great number of servants in the Hall, and their mere arrival might drive the Highwaymen away.

Yet as well as being in the House, the Earl would want to ride over the estate.

He could hardly do so with enough grooms to out-number the Highwaymen.

She thought now she had been rather remiss in not asking the Taylors how many of them there were.

However they were likely to have seen only two or three at any one time.

There might be any number of others with them in the West Wing.

"The Earl could be riding into a trap," she told herself and wondered what she could do about it.

She had now reached the Manor House.

She went first to the stables where she found the two old grooms.

She told them they were to take her father's two best carriage-horses to the "*Dog and Duck*" at Gresbury.

The grooms were obviously pleased.

"Our 'orses need exercise, Miss Vanda," the senior groom said.

"We's exercised them 's ye know," the other chimed in, "but we were only saying th' other day they be gettin' fat, an' a fat 'orse 's a lazy 'orse."

"I am sure as His Lordship wants to get home quickly, when you put them between the shafts at Gresbury, they will have to stretch themselves."

"That's what'll be good for 'em," the groom replied.

Vanda ran into the House.

Her father was working on his book and he was delighted to hear the news.

"I was wondering when that young man would be coming home," he said. "I shall look forward to talking to him."

"It will be all about the war!" Vanda protested. "You know, Papa, there is a great deal for the Earl to do on the estate, and the farmers have been asking for a long time when he will be back."

"Neil was always a good young man," Sir Alexander said, "and he proved to be an excellent soldier. I have no fears for the future."

Vanda wished she could say the same thing.

After they had finished dinner she went up to bed.

Alone she asked herself again how she could warn the Earl about the Highwaymen, and what he would do about them.

It would certainly be foolhardy for him to confront them personally.

She supposed he would think the right thing would be to contact the Barracks.

He could ask for soldiers to arrest the Highwaymen for trespassing on his estate.

She had the frightened feeling that this might end in a shooting match.

If it did, undoubtedly men would be wounded if not killed.

Then she thought that the Highwaymen would hardly be so foolish to stay in the West Wing.

As soon as they were aware that there was a great deal of activity in the Hall itself they would leave.

This meant that they might take to the woods, especially Monk's Wood, where she had first heard them.

Then the story of the Diamond Merchant returned to her mind.

Once again she felt sure that the Earl was running into danger.

"There is only one thing I can do," she decided finally, "and that is to warn him before he reaches home."

She wondered why she had not thought of that before.

If the horses were going to Gresbury, so could she.

The grooms would take them tomorrow, so that they would have a night's rest at the "*Dog and Duck*" before the Earl drove them home.

If she left on Friday as soon as it was dawn on *Kingfisher*, she could be at the Inn by breakfast-time and before the Earl left.

She thought it over carefully.

She then decided, just in case she missed him, she would ride along the side of the road for the last five miles.

He could not then pass her without her seeing him.

Early the following morning, she went up to the Hall to see what was happening.

She found Mrs. Taylor trying to organise what seemed almost an army of women.

They had arrived from the village on Mrs. Medway's instructions.

They were all gossiping excitedly about the Earl.

Vanda knew as soon as she moved among them that the Taylors had not mentioned the Highwaymen to them.

She walked round the different rooms.

Now the shutters were open, the windows cleaned, and the sunshine seeping in made the House look lovely.

She found Taylor alone in the Larder sorting out the food that was coming in from the farms.

Two young lambs, half a dozen fat ducks, a dozen chickens and a mountain of eggs!

In a low voice, just in case someone might be listening, Vanda asked:

"Have they . . gone?"

There was no need to explain who she meant.

"They be there last night, Miss Vanda," Taylor said in a conspiratorial tone.

When Vanda left him she walked to the back of the West Wing.

Moving silently through overgrown rhododendron bushes.

The lower windows were shuttered.

She stood outside one in the centre of the Wing which belonged to the principal Sitting Room.

She listened intently, thinking that if anyone moved or talked inside she was bound to hear them.

There was no sound and she prayed that the Highwaymen had taken the hint and gone.

She was not really sure if that made things better or worse.

If they were in the woods waiting for the Earl to appear, what chance would he have against armed men?

She went home more determined than ever that she must warn him before he reached the Hall.

Perhaps he would change his mind and go back to London.

Alternatively he might go first to the barracks for assistance.

She could not bear to anticipate what his reaction would be.

Yet she knew she would be doing the right thing in warning him so that he was prepared.

Sir Alexander talked about the Earl all through luncheon.

He was delighted to have lent him his horses.

He reminisced about his friendship with the old Earl and the things they had discussed when he was alive.

She thought the Earl had been very sensible in deciding to stay the last night of his journey at a Posting-Inn.

It would have spoilt the excitement of the homecoming if he had arrived late in the day.

However it made it more difficult for her to reach him.

She felt guilty in keeping her knowledge of the Highwaymen secret.

But what could her father or Mr. Rushman do themselves without help?

The answer was nothing, and she therefore felt she was entirely justified in tackling the problem on her own.

"If I save the Earl, they will all agree I have done the right thing," she told herself.

Then she sent up a little prayer to God for help.

. . . .

The Earl found it was not as easy to leave London quickly and secretly on Wednesday as he intended.

He had planned to leave for the country after breakfast.

He was however woken to be told there was a message from the Prime Minister.

57

It was too urgent to be ignored.

The Earl of Liverpool wished him to explain personally to several members of the Cabinet the latest demands of the French regarding the Army of Occupation.

Also to tell them of the Duke of Wellington's decision to send home ten thousand men.

It was impossible for the Earl to refuse such a request.

He therefore went to Downing Street, hoping he would not have to stay long.

He was over-optimistic.

The meeting went on until luncheon time and it was impossible to refuse to eat with the Prime Minister.

By the time he returned to Berkeley Square he knew he would have to postpone his departure until the following day.

It was annoying, but there was nothing he could do about it.

He therefore went to White's, to find, as he expected, several of his friends there.

"Are you going to the Devonshires' to-night?" one of them asked. "It is only a small Ball, but I always enjoy anything which is arranged by the Duchess."

"I have not made up my mind," the Earl replied evasively.

"Then someone will be very disappointed," his friend answered pointedly, "because you are sitting next to her at Carlton House."

The Earl remembered somewhat belatedly that the Prince Regent had invited him to dine with him before the Devonshires' Ball.

He had accepted.

He now decided that it was something he must refuse.

Caroline would contrive in her usual way to make people around them aware that he was her property.

To go to Carlton House would only add to the gossip which he knew was becoming dangerous.

A man could easily be pressured into marriage by social opinion.

The gossip could easily fetter him in a way that made escape impossible.

"What can I do?" he asked himself frantically.

He wished he had been able to follow his plan of leaving early that morning for Wyn Hall.

He went quickly home from White's and sat down to write a very apologetic letter to the Regent.

He had, he said, been suddenly afflicted with an extremely heavy and infectious cold.

This made it impossible for him to attend a Dinner Party.

"I am not only suffering myself," he wrote, "but I should be very remiss if I infected Your Royal Highness, when you have so many calls upon your time."

The Prince Regent was extremely fussy about his health.

The Earl knew this would ensure that his refusal to dine would be taken as an unselfish act and not an insult.

He sent a groom with it to Carlton House.

He then dined alone, having given orders that he was to be called at six o'clock next morning.

His Phaeton drawn by the best looking pair of horses he had just bought at Tattersall's was to be ready by half past.

His Valet and the luggage had already gone ahead in a Brake.

The grooms with four horses had left first thing in the morning for the Posting-Inn, where he would change horses.

Travelling with his Valet was a third groom, who was also an excellent cook.

He would see that what his master had to eat was palatable, and the Brake also carried his own wine.

The Earl thought he would be at Wyn Hall by Luncheon time the next day.

He was woken by the door of his bed-room opening, and he thought it must be a servant coming to call him.

Then as he half opened his eyes, he was aware that someone standing by his bed was lighting the candles in a silver candelabrum.

To his astonishment it was Caroline!

She had a candle in her hand which he thought must have come from one of the sconces in the passage.

"Caroline!" he exclaimed. "Why are you here at this time of night?"

She turned her face to smile at him.

He saw that she was wearing a very elaborate evening-gown and a necklace of diamonds.

"When you did not turn up at Carlton House, or at Devonshire House," she answered, "I felt I had to see you."

The Earl sat up in bed.

"You must be crazy coming here at night!" he said. "Think what the world will say when they hear about it."

"The only person who knows where I am," Caroline replied, "is your night-footman."

"And your coachman?"

Caroline shrugged her shoulders.

"They are paid not to talk, and what do servants matter?"

The Earl did not reply, but merely looked at her.

"Go away, Caroline," he said at last, "and behave yourself. You may do this sort of thing in Paris, but not in London."

"And who is to stop me:" she asked.

As she spoke he realised she was undoing the back of her gown.

While doing so her eyes were on his.

"You are behaving abominably, Caroline," he said. "You have no right to come to my house in this way and I insist on your leaving immediately."

Caroline laughed.

It was a happy sound and seemed to echo through the shadows.

Then as the Earl wondered what he could do to make her behave sensibly, she made a little movement with her body.

Her gown slithered down onto the floor.

For a moment she just stood there naked and looking in the light of the candles like a statue of Aphrodite.

Her skin was dazzlingly white and her necklace glistened iridescently.

Then before the Earl could speak or move she flung herself against him.

Her arms were round his neck, her lips on his and he felt the fiery passion of them seep through his body.

. . . .

It was nearly dawn before the Earl persuaded Caroline to leave him.

He watched her put on her gown.

He made no effort to rise himself or escort her down to the front-door.

"Will you give me luncheon?" she asked as she tidied her hair in one of the mirrors.

"I am going to the country."

"The country? Then of course I will come with you"

"No, Caroline," the Earl replied. "That is impossible."

"Why? You know I am longing to see Wyn Hall."

"I doubt if you would enjoy it, having been shut up with only Caretakers to look after it since my father died."

"We will – be together," Caroline said softly.

"There is a great deal of dust," the Earl went on, "ceilings that are leaking, beds that are damp, and of course the squeaking of mice to keep you awake."

He knew as Caroline gave a little cry that she disliked mice.

"It cannot be as bad as that!" she exclaimed.

"I expect it will be worse. When I have made everything look as it did before I went to the war, then I might consider giving a house-party."

Caroline turned to the mirror with her eyes alight.

"A house-party! I will be your hostess, darling Neil. That is a splendid idea and we will ask the Prince Regent as one of our guests. He was saying to-night at dinner it was something he would look forward to."

The Earl stiffened.

He knew exactly what Caroline had intimated when speaking of "our" guests.

If she had done so to the Prince Regent, he would believe that their engagement was just about to be announced.

His lips tightened in a hard line.

As if she was suddenly afraid she had gone too far, Caroline said:

"I did not actually say to His Royal Highness that we were engaged, but I think he suspected it."

"We are not engaged!" the Earl asserted. "As I have already told you, Caroline, I have no intention of marrying until everything I possess is as perfect as I wish it to be."

"And then I will make you the perfect wife," Caroline replied.

She moved towards the door.

"I shall expect to hear from you, darling, before the end of next week. If not, I shall come uninvited and, perhaps, bring the Regent with me."

She did not wait for the Earl's reply, but slipped out of the bed-room, closing the door behind her.

He threw himself angrily back against his pillows.

He was asking himself for the hundredth time what he could do about Caroline.

She was, the Earl knew, using every possible weapon against him.

He was not certain how he could prevent himself from being annihilated.

To use the Prince Regent as an intermediary on her behalf was, of course, a trump card.

The Regent liked to be in the know, he loved to play "cupid".

He might even, if Caroline charmed him and he was feeling generous, offer to have the Reception at Carlton House.

A wedding was just the sort of festive occasion he enjoyed.

The Earl groaned and shut his eyes.

He could see the claws of the trap, and God knows it was a man-trap, closing around him.

It would only be a question of time before he would be captured and imprisoned and there would be no escape.

Caroline would be his wife, and her lovers would eat his food, drink his wine, and sleep in his bed.

Thinking as they did so that they were fooling him.

"I cannot bear it," he murmured furiously.

He wished with all his heart he was still fighting Napoleon and the war had never ended.

CHAPTER FOUR

Sir Alexander went to his Study.

Vanda walked to the stables to speak to the grooms before they left for Gresbury.

She knew they would take the horses slowly.

She calculated that if they left at about one-thirty, they would be there soon after five.

They would go across country.

The journey took much longer by road because there were many narrow twisting lanes.

The horses were ready, looking well-groomed and, she thought, outstanding enough to please the most fastidious horse-lover.

She remembered how well the Earl had ridden as a boy.

Although she was very much younger than he was, she used to watch him admiringly.

She had a feeling that when he arrived home he would be only to glad to borrow her father's horses.

That was until he had filled his stables with his own.

The grooms touched their forelocks respectfully.

"Us be jes' off, Miss Vanda, an' us got a letter from Mr. Rushman to 'and to 'Is Lordship."

"Do not lose it," Vanda smiled.

"Us jes' 'eard a strange thing, Miss," the other groom chimed in.

Vanda turned towards him to listen and he said:

"T'boy as works in t'garden o' White Lodge tells us that early 'smarnin' 'e sees seven men on 'orseback goin' into Monk's Wood."

Vanda was suddenly still.

She knew only too well who the horsemen were.

She thought she had been very stupid.

She had not remembered when she was thinking of the Highwaymen in the West Wing that they would have horses.

This meant that they must have stabled them at the Hall.

There were a large number of empty stalls because the stables were built to hold at least fifty horses.

Now she knew, and she had never suspected it before, that the grooms also had been terrorised just as the Taylors had been.

They had therefore said nothing about the Highwaymen.

"I should have anticipated this," she thought.

Furthermore, she was horrified at learning there were more Highwaymen than she had supposed.

Seven men, all fully armed, were a formidable number for any man to encounter.

What would the Earl do about it?

She was aware that the grooms were looking at her.

They were surprised by her silence, and she asked quickly:

"I wonder who the horsemen could be?"

"Tha's wot us bin a-wonderin', Miss Vanda," the older groom said.

"While you are away, I will try to find out if anybody else has seen them," Vanda managed to say lightly, "although it seems to me the boy was dreaming."

"'E be a truthful lad," the groom said.

He was aware that Vanda was waiting for them to go.

He swung himself into the saddle of one horse and took the leading-rein of another in his left hand.

"Take them slowly," she admonished.

"Us will, Miss Vanda," the other groom replied, "'an' Jake's lookin' after t'other 'orses 'til us gets back."

Jake was his son, and nearly as experienced as his father.

Vanda watched them out of sight.

It was then she knew she must give the Earl the information where the Highwaymen were hiding.

She must also give him time to think what he could do about them.

As she walked into the house she realised that if she reached the *Dog and Duck* at Gresbury only in time to pass on her information hurriedly before he drove off on the last stage, he might run into great danger.

The Highwaymen might be planning to hold him to ransom as soon as he arrived at the Hall.

They could walk into the house when he was not expecting them.

He would certainly not be armed.

Old Buxton and the boys from the village he had taken on as footmen would have no chance of stopping them.

And the women under Mrs. Medway would merely be hysterical.

By the time Vanda reached the Drawing-Room she had decided what she should do.

It was very daring, and if anyone knew of it, it would cause a great deal of gossip.

"All that really matters is that the Earl's life is at stake," she told herself.

She went upstairs to her bed-room and selected a few things she would want for the night.

She included a light muslin gown into which she could change for dinner.

She rolled them up in a long, light bag which could be attached to *Kingfisher*'s saddle.

She changed into her best riding-habit which was a very attractive one.

Then carrying the bag and her riding-hat she went down the stairs.

She laid them down on a chair in the hall.

Then slowly, because she was nervous, went into her father's study.

Sir Alexander looked up impatiently.

He disliked being interrupted.

"I am sorry to disturb you, Papa," Vanda said, "but I have just had a message from Miss Walters. She is not at all well, and I think I should go and visit her."

Miss Walters was an old Governess who had taught Vanda for some years until she retired.

She had a cottage in a village about a mile from Gresbury.

The General knew that Vanda visited her from time to time.

"She is not well?" he exclaimed. "Well, I suppose you will have to go to her, but take Jim with you"

Jim was one of the grooms who had already left.

Vanda knew her father had forgotten for the moment that the Earl was borrowing his horses.

"I will try to be back before it gets dark," she said. "But if she keeps me too long, I will stay the night."

"I do not like your gallivanting all over the country!" Sir Alexander said crossly. "But I suppose if she has sent for you, there is nothing you can do but help her."

"It would be unkind not to, Papa," Vanda said.

She kissed her father lightly.

"Do not work too hard, and do not forget to take your medicine!"

"There is nothing wrong with me!" the General retorted.

Vanda went from the room.

She knew that once he was immersed in his book he would forget all about her.

Jake saddled *Kingfisher* and she set off.

She made a short detour so that she would not encounter the two grooms who in fact by this time were half-an-hour ahead of her.

They would be aware of how angry her father would be if he knew she was going such a long way alone.

She had no wish to tell anyone else that there were Highwaymen in the vicinity.

She knew the country over which she was riding so well that she might have been in the Park at Wyn.

She had hunted over it in the Winter, and had ridden to Gresbury dozens of times with her father.

It was quite an attractive little village.

It boasted one of the few good Posting-Inns in the County.

It was therefore not surprising that the Earl had arranged to stay there on his way home.

It was a warm, sunny day, and *Kingfisher* was enjoying the ride as much as she was.

To begin with she gave him his head.

Then they settled down to a comfortable pace which would ensure that neither of them would be too tired by the time they reached Gresbury.

They passed Savernake Forest.

It just crossed her mind to wonder whether there were more Highwaymen lurking there.

She wished the seven "Gentlemen of the Road" in Monk's Wood had preferred the vastness of Savernake to where they were at the moment.

She was, however, convinced that they would not leave Monk's Wood until they had a good haul.

Either in money or valuables from the Hall.

Once again she was thinking with horror of the miniatures, the objets d'art, the silver and gold ornaments.

They would all be easy to carry away and would fetch a good sum in a Thieves' Market.

Without really meaning to, she quickened her pace.

It was only just after five o'clock when she turned into the yard of the posting-Inn.

An Ostler came hurrying towards her, and she asked:

"Have four horses arrived belonging to General Sir Alexander Charlton?"

"No, Ma'am."

"They are not far behind," Vanda said as she dismounted, "and when the grooms arrive they will look after this horse as well."

She inspected the stables and found five stalls which she thought were superior to the others.

She ordered fresh straw and went into the Inn.

The Landlord, who was a large, burly man, bowed to her politely.

"Good-day to ye, Ma'am, and let Oi welcome ye t' the '*Dog and Duck*'."

"Thank you," Vanda replied. "I have just been explaining to your Ostler that four horses belonging to my father, General Sir Aleander Charlton, will be arriving very shortly."

The Inn-keeper looked suitably impressed as Vanda went on:

"Two of them are for the use of the Earl of Wynstock, who is, I understand, staying here to-night."

"That's right, Ma'am," the Proprietor agreed, "an' we're very 'onoured t' have 'is Lordship as our guest."

"As I have a very important message for His Lordship," Vanda said, "I wish to wait until he arrives, and I should be grateful if you would allow me to do so in your Private Parlour."

The Landlord agreed immediately.

He took Vanda down a passage which lay behind the public Dining-Room.

He showed her into a small but comfortably furnished Parlour where there was a fire burning in the grate.

A table by the window was already half-laid for dinner.

Vanda thanked him and asked if she could wash away the dust of her ride.

She was shown upstairs by a mob-capped maid.

Because her hair was slightly blown about by the wind, Vanda took off her hat with its gauze veil.

She carried it in her hand when she went downstairs.

She hoped the Earl would not be long, so that she could ride home before it got really dark.

Otherwise she would have to stay, as she had told her father, with Miss Walters.

That would be rather trying, as her Governess had become very deaf in her old age.

Almost every word had to be repeated.

Vanda had found this very exhausting the last time she had seen her.

Nevertheless she had it all well planned.

The important thing was that the Earl should know of the menace which was waiting for him when he arrived home.

. . . .

The Earl woke and realised that though it was seven o'clock he had not been called as he had ordered.

He got out of bed and rang the bell furiously.

It was always the same: when his Valet was away his orders were not carried out as precisely as he wished them to be.

Then he told himself that Croker, who had been his Batman, was a soldier.

The new servants who had just been engaged had not yet got into his ways.

A footman came hurrying in response to the bell.

The Earl demanded to know why he had not been called at six o'clock.

"I peeped in, M'Lord," the man answered, "and as Your Lordship were sound asleep, I didn't like t' trouble ye."

The way he spoke and the expression in his eyes told the Earl he was aware why he was so tired.

The rest of the household must be aware of it too.

His lips tightened.

He damned Caroline under his breath.

But he knew it was no use losing his temper and he merely said:

"Another time when I say six o'clock, I *mean* six o'clock!"

"Yes, M'Lord!"

The footman helped him dress.

There was another delay because he was quicker down the stairs than the kitchen had expected him to be.

He had therefore to wait for his breakfast.

By the time that was finished, and his Phaeton brought round from the Mews, it was after eight o'clock.

The Earl knew that to reach Gresbury that evening, he would have to drive faster than he had intended to do.

It was not that Wyn was so many miles distant from London.

It was that the roads, the Earl remembered from the past, were very bad.

It was one thing for the Prince Regent to break records when driving to Brighton.

Quite another to use the twisting, narrow lanes which had to be negotiated to reach Wyn Hall.

It was Spring, and the hedges and the banks of grass beneath them were beautiful with buds, primroses and violets.

The Earl however was concentrating on his horses.

He was too good a driver to push them and he would certainly take no unnecessary risks.

His horses were excellent and, to his relief, well-trained.

That was what he had been assured when he bought them at Tattersall's.

At the same time, it was easy when dealing with horses to be deceived.

To find, after they were delivered, that the Vendor had over-boasted his goods.

The Earl, however, was delighted with his team.

By this time he knew they were worth every penny they had cost him.

He had the good manners to stop at the Posting-Inn where he had intended to stay the first night.

He cancelled his booking, but he generously paid for it.

He had learned in France to pay for everything the British Army requisitioned from the local inhabitants.

This had astounded the French.

They had never expected to receive so much as a *cent* for their pigs, chickens and ducks from the enemy.

"Ye're a great gentlemen, M'Lord!" the Landlord of the Posting-Inn said as the Earl put a number of golden guineas down in front of him.

The Earl smiled.

Then he had driven on.

It was infuriating for one mile to be held up by a farm-cart, which it was impossible for him to pass.

It was however a very long day, having only stopped half-way to eat a very hurried meal.

He was therefore tired and extremely hungry when he turned in at the "*Dog and Duck*" at a quarter after eight.

There were two Ostlers waiting for him, and the Landlord was standing in the doorway, beaming a welcome.

"Ye've 'ad a good journey, M'Lord?"

"Not too bad," the Earl replied. "Your roads, however, are disgraceful, and something ought to be done about them!"

"Oi agree with Yer Lordship, an' every traveller says

74

th' same," the Landlord replied, "but there be nothin' we can do."

The Earl decided he would make a very strong protest to the Lord Lieutenant.

He would make it quite clear there was no reason why the roads should be so neglected.

He was sure some of them were completely impassable in Winter when there was snow or torrential rain.

He was at the moment, however, more interested in his own comfort.

The Landlord himself took him up to a bed-room, which was the best and largest in the Inn.

A small trunk which he had carried on the Phaeton was already being unpacked by the groom who had travelled with him.

As he had ordered beforehand, there was a bath set ready on the hearth-rug in front of the fire.

"Cans o' hot water'll be up in a few minutes, M'Lord," the Landlord said respectfully.

He turned to leave the room.

Then, as if he suddenly thought of it, he added:

"There be a Lady waiting for Yer Lordship downstairs. She arrived several 'ours ago."

The Earl stared at him.

He could hardly believe that Caroline could have got here before him.

"A Lady?" he questioned.

"Miss Charlton, M'Lord. Th' daughter o' General Sir Alexander Charlton, whose horses are waiting for Yer Lordship in th' stable."

The Earl relaxed.

"I understand," he said, "and of course I will apologise to the Lady for being so much later than I intended. Perhaps she will do me the honour of dining with me."

75

"I'll tell th' Lady wot Yer Lordship says."

The Landlord went from the room.

The Earl thought it was in fact a damned nuisance that he should have company at dinner.

It was the last thing he wanted.

He suspected the daughter of the General would be getting on in years.

She was obviously one of those tiresome, hard-riding women, who thought they knew more about horses than a man did.

However it seemed that he was borrowing the General's horses.

It struck him for the first time that if there were any horses left after his father's death, they would be too old to be of much use.

There would have been nobody to order Rushman to buy in new stock.

He was quick-witted enough to understand that in the circumstances Rushman had procured a team from a neighbour.

As he got into his bath the Earl was remembering the General, and that he had been a close friend of his father.

"He must be getting on in years by now," he told himself, "but his wife was a very pretty woman!"

Then he began to think once again about Caroline, and what he should do about her.

She had occupied his thoughts almost the whole way from London.

He resented that she was spoiling his home-coming to which he had been looking forward with such anticipation.

He felt rather like a small boy who had been deprived of a very exciting present.

He hated her, he told himself.

To be truthful, he had known long before he left Paris that she was everything he really disliked in a woman.

At the same time he had been weak enough to be unable to resist the fire she aroused in him.

"I have made a fool of myself," he said as he put on his evening-clothes.

He took a quick glance at himself in the mirror, then walked down the somewhat rickety oak stairs.

The Landlord was waiting for him at the bottom of them.

"Dinner'll be ready in a few minutes, M'Lord," he announced.

"I admit to being very hungry," the Earl replied.

The Landlord went ahead.

He followed him down the oak-panelled passage with its heavy beams overhead into the Parlour.

Vanda, who was waiting for him, rose as he entered.

When the Earl looked at her he was astonished.

. . . .

When she had received the Earl's invitation to dine with him, Vanda had collected her bundle from *Kingfisher's* saddle.

She had then been taken up to a bed-room where she could change.

She was glad she had brought an evening-gown with her.

It was a very simple one, which she had intended to wear at Miss Walters'.

Its high waist revealed the curves of her breast.

The hem with two simple flounces accentuated the perfection of her slim figure.

She had brought with her no adornments of any kind.

But the Earl looking at her was thinking he had never seen hair of such a strangely beautiful colour.

It was very pale, the colour of the dawn when it first appears in the sky.

As if the simile was apt, there were touches of silver like moonlight among the gold.

Because Vanda was so slim her eyes seemed to dominate her face.

They were not the blue that might have been expected with the colour of her hair.

Instead they were green – the green of the buds that the Earl had seen in the hedgerows as he drove past them.

There were also little flecks of gold which might have come from the sunshine.

He had expected a middle-aged woman, but instead he found himself face to face with a young, and very lovely girl.

Suddenly he smiled.

"Now I remember," he exclaimed. "You are Vanda!"

"I thought you would have forgotten me."

"I remember you as a very pretty child who used to ride horses that were far too big for you, and swim in the lake like a small fish!"

Varda laughed.

"And I have always remembered you taking jumps which Papa said disapprovingly were too high!"

The Earl laughed.

"My father said the same thing, but I still tried to make the impossible possible!"

They were both laughing as the Landlord hurried in with a bottle of champagne.

Vanda accepted a glass and raised her hand.

"To your Home-coming!" she said. "We have waited a long time for you."

"I, too, thought the years would never pass," the Earl said solemnly.

They sat down at the table. While the food was plain, it was well cooked.

Because the Earl was hungry, he enjoyed every mouthful.

He asked questions, and Vanda talked while they ate.

She told him how the house was in perfect repair, how Buxton and Mrs. Medway had come back.

"It may not be in quite as perfect order as it was when your father was alive," she said, "but they are doing their best with very little notice."

The Earl heard the reproachful note in her voice, and he said:

"I know it was inconvenient. At the same time, I wanted to leave London at short notice. As it was, I was delayed at the last minute, and only left this morning."

"Then you have been travelling all day!" Vanda remarked.

The Earl nodded.

"You were very lucky. During the winter months it sometimes take three days for anyone to reach us."

Once again the Earl was talking about the roads.

The last course was served and the Earl had accepted a glass of brandy.

It was so good he was certain it had been smuggled.

The servants withdrew and they were alone.

They moved from the table to sit in two arm-chairs in front of the fire.

Large logs were burning cheerfully, and it was very warm and inviting.

However it was growing late.

Vanda knew she must hurry and tell the Earl why she had come.

Otherwise by the time she reached Miss Walters' cottage, she might be asleep.

"What is worrying you?" the Earl asked.

"I was thinking that I must talk quickly, otherwise my old Governess, who lives in the next village and is not expecting me, will not hear me knocking."

"You mean – you are not staying here?"

"Of course not!" Vanda said. "I came to see you because it was urgent. If you had not been so late, I had expected to ride home before it was dark."

The Earl looked at her. Then he asked:

"Why did you have to see me, apart from bringing me your father's horses?"

"They were coming without me."

The Earl put down his glass.

"Then what is it that you have to tell me?" he enquired.

He was aware perceptively that, unlike most women, she had not been waiting for him just for the pleasure of his company.

"Things are happening at Wyn Hall which are very serious," Vanda said.

She instinctively lowered her voice as she spoke.

The Earl looked at her, but he did not speak.

She went on:

"It is going to upset you and spoil your home-coming. At the same time, I have to warn you."

"To – warn me?"

"That you may be in grave danger!"

The Earl looked bewildered.

"Why – and from whom:"

Vanda drew in her breath.

"For some days now the West Wing has been occupied by a band of Highwaymen!"

The Earl sat upright and his expression was incredulous.

"Did you say – Highwaymen? In the West Wing? I do not believe it!"

"It is true," Vanda said. "They have terrorised the Taylors, who are your Caretakers, and I think, although I have not spoken to them, that they have also threatened the grooms."

"Why has no one done anything about it?" the Earl asked. "Surely, Rushman . . ?"

"Mr. Rushman does not know," Vanda interrupted. "'Nor does my father. In fact, I am the only person, apart from the servants concerned, who are aware that they are there."

"It seems extraordinary that they should go into the house!"

"The house has been empty," Vanda pointed out, "and I have been terrified lest they should ransack the many precious things that it contains."

"Why do you think they have not already done so?"

Vanda hesitated, then she thought the Earl had better hear the truth.

"What I fear," she said, "although I have no foundation for it, is that they need money and intend to extort it from you, if you return!"

"*If* I return?" the Earl repeated. "Are you seriously suggesting I should not do so?"

"I think it might be dangerous, unless you have Military protection."

"I have never heard such nonsense!" the Earl said scornfully. "And I can assure you, Vanda, I am not afraid of a couple of Highwaymen!"

"There are seven of them," Vanda said quietly, "and from the terror they have evoked in the Taylors, I think they must be very dangerous men!"

"This is certainly something I did not expect," the Earl said. "Do you really think they might injure me?"

"Years ago Papa told me how a Highwayman called Watson extorted money from a Diamond Merchant, who subsequently died as a result of the rough way he had been treated."

"I had forgotten that story," the Earl said, "but that was in the last century, and actually I did not think of Highwaymen being Kidnappers."

"Then you have forgotten Captain James Campbell and Sir John Johnson," Vanda replied.

"What did they do?"

"They abducted a girl of thirteen who was an heiress and James Campbell forced her to marry him."

"Good Heavens!" the Earl exclaimed. "Did she escape?"

"The Highwaymen were caught," Vanda replied, "and Sir John was hanged but Captain Campbell escaped by going abroad."

The Earl did not speak and Vanda went on:

"I am sure there are just as many Highwaymen, robbers and thieves now as there were then, especially with so many men being demobilised, without money and without work."

The Earl knew this was true, and was what he had seen for himself.

There was silence until he asked:

"What do you suggest I do?"

Vanda smiled.

"I came to warn you to be prepared, not to make decisions for you. After all, you are the soldier!"

"At least I knew where my enemy was," the Earl said.

"I told you . . at the moment they are in Monk's Wood."

"And you think they will stay there?"

"I cannot be sure, but I think it very likely as they know you are coming home."

"I suppose that is the obvious thing to think," the Earl agreed. "But what can I do?"

"I have already suggested you should go to the Barracks, and ask the Officer in Charge to send a Company of men to Wyn Hall."

The Earl considered this for some seconds.

Then he said:

"I suppose, really, I dislike having to admit that I am helpless. Are there no able-bodied men on the estate?"

"There are a few," Vanda admitted, "but most of them, as they have not been in the war, do not know how to shoot, and a pitchfork is not very efficient against a bullet."

The Earl slapped his hands down on the arms of his chair.

"It is intolerable!" he exclaimed. "The situation is as bad as it was fifty years ago! I remember my grandmother telling me that the streets were so dangerous when she was a girl that when she and her mother moved to and from Court in sedan chairs they had to be escorted by servants carrying blunderbusses to protect them from the robbers!"

Vanda laughed.

"At least you can move quicker than that!"

She paused before she said:

"I cannot help thinking that if your horses had been better than theirs, they would have taken yours with them!"

"I suppose you are right," the Earl agreed rather reluctantly. "But I have to admit it is humiliating that I cannot protect myself and my staff and am obliged to ask help from the Military."

"It would be far more humiliating to be tied up and forced to give them an enormous sum of money!" Vanda said practically.

"That is true. Very well, I will not go straight home, as I had intended, but drive to the Barracks."

Vanda clasped her hands together.

"I am so glad you think that is a sensible thing to do. Now I must go!"

She rose to her feet, and the Earl said:

"Do not be stupid, Vanda! Look at the time!"

There was a clock on the mantelpiece, and when Vanda looked at it she was horrified to find that it was after eleven o'clock.

She stared at it, thinking it must be incorrect, but the Earl said:

"Stay here. I am sure you are not nervous at being with me."

"No, of course not!" Vanda replied. "I am only thinking of my reputation . . and of course . . yours!"

The Earl laughed.

"No one would be surprised to hear I was accompanied by a beautiful Lady, and you are in fact very beautiful!"

She blushed, and he thought she looked exceedingly lovely as she did so.

"Thank you," she said. "That is the first compliment I have had for a long time."

"Is everybody blind in Little Stock?" the Earl enquired.

Vanda's eyes twinkled.

"No, My Lord, they are old!"

"I never thought of that," the Earl said. "Of course, all the young men, like myself, must have gone to the war."

"All of them!" Vanda said softly. "And some will never come back."

There was a little tremor in her voice.

"Well, you shall listen to my compliments," the Earl said, "and as soon as the house is livable, I will produce my friends from London, who can be far more eloquent than I am."

"Your Lordship is very kind," Vanda replied, "but at the moment I am more concerned with Highwaymen!"

"If you call me 'My Lord' again, I think I shall spank you!" the Earl said. "We were brought up together, and my name, in case you have forgotten it, is Neil."

"I am well aware of that," Vanda said, "but I thought it would be a mistake to presume on a childhood friendship."

Before he could speak she added:

"No, that is the wrong word – childhood adoration. I thought you were all the heroes in the History Books, besides undoubtedly being the reincarnation of a Greek god!"

The Earl threw back his head and laughed.

"Until I became the age you are now, I thought all girls were a nuisance!"

As he spoke he thought they still were, if they were anything like Caroline.

She was certainly beautiful.

Yet at the moment he was thinking that Vanda outshone her in a very different way with a beauty that was unique.

Aloud he said:

"Now be sensible, and take a room here for the night. You will have to come with me to-morrow to the Barracks to explain exactly what is happening at Wyn Hall. As I have never been there, they may not listen to me."

"I think that is unlikely," Vanda smiled. "Everyone in the County knows how important you have been to the Duke, and the medal you received after Waterloo."

"Oh – that!" the Earl exclaimed.

"Yes, that!" Vanda echoed. "You will find even in peacetime it counts for a great deal!"

"Then by the authority I gained during the war," the Earl said, "you will, Vanda, take your orders from me!"

He smiled at her beguilingly and added:

"I will explain to the Inn-Keeper that my being so late has prevented you from going on to where you were staying. I will tell him you need one of his best rooms with a maid servant next door in the dressing room."

"I think no one could object to that," Vanda said.

"The important thing is for no one to know about it," the Earl remarked. "We will leave early in the morning and, as you suggested, go straight to the Barracks."

He thought for a moment, then said:

"Perhaps it would be a mistake for us to ride into

the village together. We must therefore tell the grooms who will be riding my horses to wait at a place where I can drop you before I go on to the Hall."

Vanda looked at him approvingly.

"Now you are taking charge!" she said. "And that is exactly what I wanted you to do!"

"And now, as we are both tired," the Earl said, "we will go to bed as soon as I have seen the Landlord."

He walked from the room as he spoke.

Vanda felt as if the burden she had carried on her shoulders ever since she had spoken to the Taylors had lightened.

She was afraid, desperately afraid, that the Highwaymen would rob the house or injure the Earl.

But at least she had been able to persuade him to ask for assistance.

She was saying a little prayer of thankfulness when he came back into the Parlour.

"Everything is arranged," he said, "so now you can stop worrying about me."

He stood looking at her in a manner which made her raise her eye-brows enquiringly.

"I am wondering how I can thank you," he said, "for taking such good care of me."

He knew exactly how any other woman would have responded.

But Vanda merely said quickly:

"Keep your fingers crossed! We have a long way to go before you are really safe, and I can only go on praying that you will be clever enough to outwit the enemy."

The Earl took her hand in his.

"Thank you, Vanda," he said, "I need your prayers."

Because he was grateful to her, and also because

he had been in France, his lips touched the softness of her skin.

He saw the surprise in her eyes.

He also felt the little quiver that went through her.

CHAPTER FIVE

The Earl came down to breakfast early to find Vanda already in the parlour.

She was looking very smart in her riding-habit wearing a hat which had a gauze veil trailing behind it.

"Good-morning, Vanda!" he smiled. "Now I know you really are a country-girl!"

"Because I am up so early?" Vanda asked. "I like riding when the world is fresh."

"So do I," the Earl agreed, "and I wish I was riding this morning."

As the Landlord and the waitresses came hurrying in with their breakfast he said:

"As I want to talk to you on the way to where we are going, I have told my groom to ride your horse."

He thought Vanda looked as if she was going to refuse, and added quickly:

"He is a very experienced rider, and I promise you, you can trust him."

"I am sure I can," Vanda said, "and actually Papa's grooms with your team have already left."

"I thought they would have," the Earl said, "and if they have to wait for you so that you can ride home with them, I am sure that will present no difficulties."

89

Vanda had already told the grooms to take the Earl's superlative horses as gently as possible.

They were to meet her at the crossroads.

It was about a mile from the village, and she doubted if there would be any people about to notice them.

She knew her father, when they arrived home, would be extremely interested in the Earl's new horses.

She thought with a little feeling of excitement that it would be wonderful when the stables at the Hall were filled with horses to equal them.

Now as they went on with their breakfast the Earl asked:

"Did you sleep well?"

"Very well, thanks to you."

There was a question in his eyes and she explained:

"I have been worrying about you, riding blithely into danger. But now that you are going to the Barracks, I am no longer afraid."

"I am longing to say," he answered, "that the whole situation is exaggerated! I cannot really believe that English Highwaymen, however many there may be, are anything like as intimidating as Napoleon Bonaparte!"

Vanda laughed. Then she said:

"One is a National problem, the other a personal one."

The Earl liked the quick way she managed to reply to him, and he said:

"After what you told me last night about the distressing lack of compliments paid in this part of the country, may I tell you that you look very lovely, and very smart!"

"You are making me feel as if I were deliberately asking for compliments," Vanda replied, "but now they are here, I am definitely enjoying them."

The Earl laughed.

Vanda could not help feeling that it was very exciting to be with him.

When breakfast was finished, the Earl paid the Inn-Keeper so generously that he bowed almost to the ground in appreciation of what he had received.

Outside the Earl's Phaeton was waiting.

When his groom had handed him the reins he started to move out of the yard.

The groom mounted *Kingfisher* and followed them.

Vanda knew the way to the Barracks, but the Earl, having been away for so long, was not certain.

He could not go very fast, owing to the lanes twisting and turning.

Or places so narrow that if they met a cart or a wagon one of them would have to go back.

To Vanda's delight the Earl was ready to talk about his experiences in France.

Best of all, he told her how brilliant the Duke of Wellington had been.

"No one else," he said positively, "could have succeeded in defeating Bonaparte."

"That is what we all felt," Vanda said.

"He is the hero of all Europe," the Earl went on, "and when he comes home for good next year, I am only hoping this country will show its appreciation."

"I hope so, too," Vanda replied. "He is a very great man!"

"And I am extremely lucky to have been associated with him this last year," the Earl said.

Vanda liked the way he spoke almost humbly.

He was obviously reluctant to talk about his own achievements.

Then the Barracks loomed ahead of them.

She thought sadly that perhaps never again would she have a chance of such an intimate conversation with the Earl.

They drove up to the gates.

He said who he was and informed the sentry that he wished to speak to the Officer in Charge.

"That'll be Major Lawson, Sir," the sentry replied.

He pointed the way to the centre building and the Earl drove his horses up to it.

There they had to wait until the groom who had been riding *Kingfisher* could find a soldier to hold him.

When he did the man went to the head of the team.

The Earl helped Vanda to alight.

They walked in through an imposing door with two sentries at attention as they did so.

When the Earl again said who he was, he was taken immediately to Major Lawson's office.

He was a middle-aged man, looking smart and efficient in his uniform.

He greeted the Earl enthusiastically.

"This is a very great honour, My Lord!" he said. "In fact I did not know that you had returned to England."

"I have only just got back," the Earl answered.

"Then I can only say how very glad we are to see you:" Major Lawson replied.

"Thank you," the Earl said, "and now may I introduce you to Miss Charlton, who I think you may be aware is the daughter of General Sir Alexander Charlton."

"I do not think we have met," the Major said to Vanda as he shook her hand, "but I know your father, and have a great admiration for him."

"Thank you," Vanda said.

"We have come to see you on an important matter," the Earl said, "and I should be obliged, Major, if we could talk to you in private."

The Major looked surprised, but he said:

"Of course!"

He turned to the young Lieutenant who was working at another desk in the room and said:

"See that we are not disturbed."

"Very good, Sir!" the Lieutenant replied.

He walked from the room closing the door quietly behind him.

The Earl and Vanda sat down on two chairs near the Major's desk.

As they did so Major Lawson asked:

"Now, what can I do for you, My Lord?"

"I think Miss Charlton can explain it better than I could do," the Earl replied.

He looked at Vanda as he spoke who said:

"When I learned that the Earl was returning to Wyn Hall, I contacted him very early this morning to warn him of the danger . . "

"The danger?" Major Lawson asked in surprise.

"Seven Highwaymen have been occupying the West Wing, and are terrorising the Caretakers and the grooms."

For a moment the Major stared at her in astonishment before he exclaimed:

"So that is where the Baker Gang are hanging out!"

"The Baker Gang?" the Earl repeated. "Do you mean you have been looking for them?"

"For the last two months," Major Lawson replied. "We were warned by the Barracks in Warwickshire that they were on their way, and we thought they were in Savernake Forest."

"And you have been trying to capture them?"

"So far they have managed to conceal their exact whereabouts," Major Lawson replied. "But they are very dangerous and a menace to the countryside. In fact their criminal record is the worst of any Highwaymen I have ever encountered."

The way the Major spoke made Vanda give a little exclamation of horror.

The Earl bent forward to say:

"Tell me about them."

"The leader," Major Lawson said, "a man called Baker, was once a Pastry Cook. He had a shop in Mayfair and was patronised by the aristocracy – who bankrupted him:"

The Earl looked surprised, and the Major explained:

"His clients ran up large bills and eventually, when they did not settle them, he could carry on no longer."

The Major paused for a moment. Then he said:

"As you can imagine, this gave him a grudge against society, and he vowed he would avenge himself."

"So he took to the road!" the Earl exclaimed.

"Exactly:" Major Lawson agreed. "He and his Gang have not only murdered a great number of people, but also tortured them!"

"Oh, no!" Vanda exclaimed involuntarily.

"I am afraid it is true, Miss Charlton," the Major said. "Baker prefers cash to valuables, and in several instances, having sent a ransom note to his victim's relatives, if the money is not forthcoming immediately, he has sent them a finger, a toe, or an ear, to speed up the payment!"

Vanda drew in her breath and clutched her fingers together.

She was looking not at the Major, but at the Earl, and after a moment he said:

"You were quite right, Vanda, in making me come here!"

"This is Miss Charlton's doing?" the Major asked. "Then I can only assure Your Lordship that you are not dealing with Story-Book 'Gentlemen of the Road', but a monster, and the world will be a better place once he is out of it!"

"I can understand that," the Earl said.

"Baker and those who follow him also have an unpleasant habit when they have taken a prisoner of putting out his eyes so that he cannot identify them."

Aware that what the Major was saying was upsetting Vanda, the Earl said:

"You have told me enough, Major, to assure me that I was right in coming to you for protection, and Miss Charlton can tell you where the Gang are at the moment."

The Major picked up his pen and Vanda said:

"They have left the West Wing at Wyn Hall now and were seen by a boy, who told my father's grooms, going into Monk's Wood."

"It is a long time since I was at Wyn Hall," the Major said, "but I think I am right in believing that Monk's Wood is a little South of the house."

"That is right," Vanda said. "It is a large, rambling wood and no one in the village will go there, which I am sure is why they have chosen it."

She thought the Major looked puzzled and explained:

"Monk's Wood was named after a Priest who left his Priory and settled in the wood to pray and minister to the animals who came to him when they were injured."

"Now you mention it," Major Lawson said, "I seem to remember hearing the story."

"In the very centre of the wood, which is where I think the Gang will be, are the remains of the Chapel he built, and where it is said he administered the Mass not only to any traveller who happened to find his way there, but also to the deer, the foxes, the hares, the rabbits and the birds who trusted him to mend their injuries."

"So that is the story!" Major Lawson exclaimed. "Then the sooner we can get those fiends out of such a Holy place, the better!"

"I agree with you," Vanda replied. "I have always loved riding in Monk's Wood because it has an atmosphere which I believe lingers on, even though the Monk has been dead for two hundred years."

She spoke with a touching sincerity and the Earl smiled at her as if he understood.

"Now, what I suggest," Major Lawson said, "is that His Lordship stays here to-night."

"To-night?" the Earl asked sharply.

"It is extremely unfortunate," Major Lawson explained, "but at the moment practically every soldier in the Barracks is out on manoeuvres. Some of them will be returning at about five o'clock to-day, but the rest will not report in until to-morrow morning."

The Earl's lips tightened, but Vanda, knowing there was nothing else he could do, said quietly:

"You must stay. It would be madness to go back to the Hall now we know what those men are like."

"I agree with you, Miss Charlton," Major Lawson said, "and I can assure you, M'Lord, we will make you as comfortable as possible. My wife and I will be very honoured if you will stay at our house, which I hope would be more comfortable than the Barracks!"

He gave a little laugh before he added:

"All the same, you are certainly used to them."

"I am indeed," the Earl replied, "and I was looking forward to being in my own house."

"Of course you were," Major Lawson replied, "but I cannot stress too strongly how dangerous it would be for you to go there alone. I am sure Miss Charlton is right in thinking the Baker Gang are only waiting for your return."

"Very well," the Earl agreed reluctantly, "I must do as you say."

"What you and I will do, My Lord," Major Lawson said, "is to work out the best plan of attack, which means, I think, approaching the wood simultaneously from every angle so that there is no possibility of their being able to escape."

"If it comes as a surprise, it will, I hope, prevent a lot of bloodshed," the Earl said.

"That is what I hope," Major Lawson said, "and, My Lord, as you are far more experienced than I am in fighting a battle, I shall certainly bow to your superior judgement in anything we do."

"Thank you," the Earl said quietly.

There was a little pause. Then Vanda said:

"I will go home and tell everybody that His Lordship has been delayed in London. The only people who will know he spent the night at the 'Dog and Duck' at Gresbury are my father's grooms, who are absolutely trustworthy."

"If you will do that, Miss Charlton," Major Lawson said, "it would be a very great help, and give us a chance to take these felons off their guard."

Vanda rose to her feet.

"My horse is outside," she said, "and I will leave at once."

Then she hesitated and said to the Earl:

"I had better put your horses into Papa's stable, where no one will see them. If they go to the Hall your grooms will know that you are not still in London, and the Highwaymen will get to hear of it."

"That is sensible of you," the Earl agreed.

Vanda held out her hand to Major Lawson.

"Good-bye, Major," she said. "I only pray that all this horror will soon be over, and His Lordship can enjoy his home-coming in peace."

"I promise you, Miss Charlton, that my men will do their best," Major Lawson answered, "and I shall be looking forward to seeing your father again."

Vanda smiled at him.

Then the Earl said:

"I will see Miss Charlton off, then return, Major, to go into our plans in detail."

The Major nodded his agreement, and did not leave his desk.

The Earl escorted Vanda outside to where a soldier was holding *Kingfisher*.

"For God's sake, Vanda," he said in a low voice, "take care of yourself, and do not take any risks."

"No, of course not."

She knew he was thinking of her telling him how she had first become aware of the Highwaymen.

He lifted her into the saddle and arranged her skirt neatly over the stirrup.

When he had done so he looked up at her and their eyes met.

"There is no need for me to tell you that you have been wonderful!" he said quietly.

"All that matters is that you are safe," Vanda replied.

They were looking into each other's eyes, and somehow it was very difficult to look away.

Then with an effort Vanda lifted the reins and turned *Kingfisher*'s head towards the gate.

She was aware as she went that the Earl was watching her, but she did not look back.

She was already praying that he would work out a plan by which as few men as possible would be in danger.

She had, however, the uncomfortable feeling that if there was going to be a battle with the Highwaymen, the Earl would be in the thick of it.

It was some distance to the crossroads from the Barracks, but the grooms were there waiting.

As she drew nearer to them Vanda thought it would be impossible to find finer horses anywhere than those the Earl had recently purchased.

As she drew up beside them the grooms touched their forelocks.

They were obviously pleased to see her.

"These be real foin 'orses, Miss Vanda!" one of them said. "We're 'opin' the Master, when he sees 'em, will be lookin' for somethin' like 'em for our stables."

"We will show them to him," Vanda said, "because we are taking them home with us, and not to the stables at the Hall."

The two grooms looked at her in surprise.

They started to ride slowly in the direction of the village.

Then Vanda told them about the Highwaymen in the wood and that the Earl was in grave danger.

"That be roight terrible news, Miss Vanda!" the older groom said.

"I know," Vanda agreed, "and we have to play our part in keeping the secret until the Highwaymen are all captured."

She then told them that they had to make everybody in the village believe that the Earl had stayed in London.

He had not met them as they had expected him to do, at Gresbury.

"You set off with four horses and came back with four," Vanda insisted so that the grooms would get the story into their minds, "and unless anyone looks into our stables, they will have not the slightest idea that two of the horses are not the Master's."

"Oi sees wot ye mean," the younger groom said. "An' we're t'tell everyone as asks uns that 'Is Lordship be still in London."

"That is right," Vanda said in a tone of relief. "And it is very, very important that everybody in the village believes you."

"An' wot 'bout them up at t' 'All?" the older groom enquired.

"I will tell Buxton and Mrs. Medway exactly the same tale," Vanda replied.

．　．　．　．　．　．　．

Vanda and the grooms arrived home having been careful not to go through the village.

They had approached the Manor from the far side so that no one saw the horses.

Vanda gave *Kingfisher* to Jake, who was waiting for them.

Then she went into the house.

Her father, as she expected, was already in his Study.

He looked up with a smile when she entered the room.

"You are back, my dear!" he said. "I worried when you did not return last night."

"I was afraid you might, Papa," Vanda replied, "but something very, very important has happened about which I must tell you."

She shut the door and pulled off her hat.

Sitting down in front of him she told her father the whole story of the Highwaymen.

Sir Alexander listened in astonishment.

"Why did you not tell me before?" he asked.

"Because, Papa, it would have worried you, and there was nothing you could do about their being in the West Wing, and it was for the same reason that I did not tell Mr. Rushman."

"I think we should both have known!" Sir Alexander asserted. "I should have sent to the Barracks immediately."

"They might somehow have got away," Vanda said quietly. "But now the Earl is in charge, and I am sure they can be captured, which Major Lawson has been trying to do for several months."

"It is absolutely disgraceful that this sort of thing should be happening!" Sir Alexander said angrily. "And the Army so incompetent that they have been unable to bring these felons to justice!"

This was the sort of attitude, Vanda thought, that her father would take.

At the same time, there had been few soldiers left in the country.

Also in a County like Wiltshire, where there were so

many forests, it was not really difficult for a few men on horseback to be able to hide themselves.

Aloud she said:

"You do understand, Papa, that no one is to know anything about this except yourself until after to-morrow? I am going up to the Hall to tell them that you have had a message from London to say that the Earl has been detained, and will be returning later in the week. Somehow I expect the Highwaymen will hear of it."

"I blame the Taylors," Sir Alexander stormed, "for being too chicken-hearted to inform anyone in authority what has been going on."

"The Taylors are absolutely terrified," Vanda said, "and now we know what monsters these particular Highwaymen are, one cannot really blame them."

Her father was silent, and she added:

"You have never told me stories of Highwaymen who were cruel enough to put out their victim's eyes, or to send fingers and toes to those from whom they were demanding a ransom!"

"It is not the sort of thing one would tell a child!" Sir Alexander replied. "And I agree with you, my dear, the sooner the Baker Gang are hanged at Tyburn, the better!"

"That is true, Papa," Vanda said. "But you have for-gotten that Highwaymen are no longer publicly hanged at Tyburn as they were in the past. It was a horrible and barbaric practice with the whole place looking like a Fairground, with side-shows and street vendors!"

"It was disgraceful," Sir Alexander admitted, "and I remember as a boy hearing gruesome tales of the society women who waited there as if the place was a Playhouse!"

"Now the gallows are in the court-yard at the Old Bailey," Vanda said. "The procession and the Fairground have been done away with, but the hanging is still open to the public."

"Where criminals are concerned I agree with that as a deterrent," Sir Alexander said firmly.

Vanda picked up her hat and walked towards the door.

It was justice, and certainly the Baker Gang deserved to die for their crimes.

Yet she did not like to think of any man however bad being hanged by the neck until he was no longer breathing!

After lunching with her father, and they were very careful what they said in front of Dobson, Sir Alexander returned to his Study.

It was then Vanda decided to go to the Hall.

Kingfisher was saddled for her, and she entered the Park by the gate she always used.

Then she trotted under the oak trees towards the lake.

She was thinking of the Earl.

She knew how frustrated he must feel having to stay in the Barracks, and not being able to come home until to-morrow.

She had realised that every instinct in his body rebelled against Major Lawson's decision.

At the same time, his brain told him he would be very foolish to do anything else.

'The Earl is too good a soldier to take any unnecessary risks,' Vanda thought.

She rode up to the front-door of Wyn Hall.

Buxton must have seen her approach for a footman came running down the steps to hold *Kingfisher*'s head.

Another footman helped Vanda to dismount.

It was something she could easily have done herself.

But she appreciated that Buxton was teaching the footmen the correct way of behaving when guests arrived.

He greeted her as she walked up the steps and she said:

"Good-afternoon, Buxton. The General has asked me to bring you some news, which I am afraid you will find disappointing."

"Disappointing, Miss Vanda?" Buxton enquired.

"Yes, a messenger arrived from London to tell my father that His Lordship has been detained, I think by the Prime Minister, and he will therefore not come to-day, as was expected, but as soon as he possibly can."

"Oh, dear!" Buxton exclaimed. "Chef'll be disappointed! He's got everything ready for a special dinner to-night for His Lordship!"

"That is what I expected would happen," Vanda said, "but of course, as His Lordship has just returned from France, it is understandable that many important people wanted to see him as soon as he got home."

"I suppose we'll just 'ave to wait our turn," Buxton said. "I only hopes it's not for long!"

"From what His Lordship wrote to my father," Vanda replied, "he is as disappointed as you are, but we think in fact he may turn up to-morrow."

"Then that's what we'll look forward to," Buxton said.

As if he wanted Vanda to appreciate the improvements that had been made at the Hall he said:

"I wonder, Miss Vanda, if you'd just take a look at